# A Vision of Neon

# A Vision of Neon

## Angela M. Graziano

**SERVING HOUSE BOOKS**

A Vision of Neon

ISBN: 978-0-9838289-7-6

Cover design: *the*BookDesigners

Cover image © Photocase/*redsocks*

Author photo: Kay English

Serving House Books logo by Barry Lereng Wilmont

Published by Serving House Books
Copenhagen, Denmark and Florham Park, NJ

www.servinghousebooks.com

First Serving House Books Edition 2012

# Author's Note

My intent in writing this work of creative nonfiction has been to create an impressionistic rendering of these two women's lives; to make sense of events that were impossible for me to understand when I was young; to find meaning in moments that once seemed otherwise meaningless; to put emphasis on the friendship and the journey and not only on what happened in the end. In order to accomplish that, some scenes have been compressed or excluded. Many of the names of people and places have been changed.

*For Megan*

I try to think back to the beginning of things. To those moments that seem like images from a stranger's life.

When I am not looking, I always find them: the tiny reminders, the pieces of proof, that confirm that life was my own. While organizing storage, while digging to the bottoms of drawers, while searching beneath my bed, they present themselves to me: the dusty memories I hide from.

When people ask me how long I knew Kelsey was ill, my answer often varies. Sometimes, I say a year, sometimes five years, sometimes forever and other times I say only for a moment, right towards the end. I try to place my finger on it. Attempt to sort through the mess in my head, carve a path through the clutter and find the minute it all came crashing down. That solitary second that would enable me to place blame, to find a reason, to understand how it all went slip-sliding away from me.

I try to remember the beginning of it all.

"I found a doctor," my mother confesses to me through the phone. "I think you should go see her. I think you should find someone to talk to."

"I don't need to talk to anyone," I lie. "I'm fine. Look, I have a big final exam tomorrow and I really need to —"

"She's gone, Angela," my mother interrupts. "Next week will be one year. You have to finally admit that she's not coming back. You have to stop pretending that just because you're hours away at college that she is still here waiting for you to come home."

Her words, like so many other factors in my day-to-day routine, pierce me and deflate me of breath. In just seconds, I lose control of my body as my daily battle with acute panic begins. My fingertips burn from the invisible needles that stab them. A rush of tiny bumps spreads across my chest. I press my fingers to my neck in order to ensure I am alive. My pulse thuds. I rest on my bed with the intention of sitting for only a moment, but before I can lift myself from the mattress it becomes impossible to breathe.

I gulp for air.

I'm certain I'll never have enough of it. Certain I'll die here, in this dorm room, alone. Or worse, that I'll be fine and instead God will inexplicably kill every person I've ever loved. My mind forces violent fantasies upon me in which the end result is always the brutal fictional deaths of those closest to me — vivid images of their bodies splayed lifelessly just out of my reach. My body feels like it will convulse, only the opposite happens. I become immobile. I am a statue, unable to move for fear that I will fall and shatter and become entirely unglued.

"You need to accept this, Angela," my mother says. "You need to feel the pain of it. It's like your mind has blocked all your memories of her. You just pretend the whole thing — your whole life with her — never happened. Until you accept the fact that she's dead, you will never live."

I gulp for air.

"Just make the appointment," I whisper. "I'll try to squeeze it in next week while I'm home for the holiday."

A door opens and the doctor's voice spills into the room — this woman who has promised to change everything. With a few magic words she will make it all go away. Like some black magic shaman she will make the bogeyman, the sandman, and the monster in the closet all disappear. *Poof.* And just like that, the curse will be over and order will be restored.

I continue to flip the pages of my magazine.

The doctor is not how I had imagined. She does not wear practical heels or a sharply tailored suit as I thought she would, but rather, loose pants and chunky clogs. A man, who I assume to be another patient, walks out behind her. He brushes past me and parts his lips into a thin, straight smile. It is the sort of respectful smile you offer a passerby in a hospital corridor, a graveyard or a place like this. The type of smile that silently swears life will go on.

I am invited inside the doctor's office. Until now, nearly every time I've visited a doctor's office it has been to treat a scratched elbow or a common flu. I imagine the interior will have the same cold floor, buzzing florescent bulbs and thumb-tacked diagrams I am used to seeing. I envision myself hopping onto the metal table and crinkling a sheet of white tissue beneath me. I will stick out my tongue and let this sense of sickness pour from my insides. When I am healed, the doctor will offer me a fruit-flavored lollipop and pat my knee.

"You have been so brave," she will say through a smile.

The office emits a sense of warmth I had not expected. Votive candles flicker like fireflies; plush, cushioned sofas line the walls I imagined would be busy with chrome biohazard bins; crystals dangle from rafters and window frames and send miniature rainbows dancing across the room. I take a seat, allow my body to sink into the thick upholstery, and stare silently out the window. Through the windowpane yellow sunlight catches a crystal that hangs from the frame. I gaze at the icy formations opposite the glass; they drip in perfectly precise illuminated points that remind me of props from a movie set. The world I see is covered in a perfect blanket of glittering Hollywood snow.

When I was younger, I did not believe in the idea of memories fading. I was certain my mind would forever be full of the laughter, the scents, and the sounds of complete days. Like a wicked sunburn that never really disappears, but instead, leaves behind permanent speckles of browned skin.

I was wrong.

Many of my memories have floated away and become particles that I feel but cannot see. In their places, only splinters remain. Slices of moments. Narrow slivers from much larger days. At some point, when I was not looking, my memories — my life — transformed into a series of scenes.

The doctor sits across from me and slides her shoes from her feet. She tucks her legs beneath her rounded bottom. I stare out the window and view snow as it floats delicately to the earth, and see the rushing black car tires that spin past, turning the beauty of the street to a muted gray. I can feel the doctor watch me, can feel the invisible energy of her eyes as they observe each of my breaths. I pretend to be oblivious. I know that soon, she will speak, and our session will begin.

I gaze at the accumulating flakes. They glisten as they drift gracefully toward the ground. I want so badly to concentrate on their brilliance. To find a source of peace on this numbing winter day. But all I can think of is how I'd like to jump from my chair and shake the doctor by her shirtsleeves. About how I'd like to cup my hand across her lips and beg her to stay silent.

The moment she speaks is the moment all of this will become real for me.

For so long, I have played a game of hide and seek with myself, running from the truth, crouching behind sofas, my eyes covered to avoid the answers.

Tag.

Now I am it.

The doctor has found me and the game is done.

She places her papers down beside her and clears her throat.

Through the window I believe I see two children dance in the winter landscape. They toss handfuls of the snow into the air, and twirl beneath the white, shimmering dust. I blink and, in an instant, the image of them is gone.

I lower my eyelids and think of her — this friend I can no longer see. Images of her pulse through my mind like a static slideshow against a wall of darkness. The memories come back in broken, fragmented bits that I pray will eventually form a whole. Like snowflakes that fall one by one and, in time, create a perfect storm.

"Would you like to get started?" the doctor asks.

I gulp for air.

And in this instant, I begin to remember it all.

# The Beginning

# 1994.

Seventh grade. The first period bell will ring soon. Hallways will flood with a rush of students who wave assignments above their heads, book bags slapping backs while feet scuff and squeal across the floor. Classroom doors will shut, a final metal locker will slam, teacher's hands and forearms will become white with chalk dust, surnames misread from attendance sheets. Everyone please stand.

*With liberty and justice for all.*

The start to another day.

For now, the bathroom bustles with teenage girls. Lanky twelve-and-thirteen-year old bodies press against porcelain sinks, shove toward the mirrors to study reflections, and glide pearl-pink frosted lip-gloss across strawberry-tinted lips. Gossip is exchanged. Small talk about nothing. About everything. I hardly hear any of it.

Kelsey sits on a green radiator, swings her legs and kicks her black lace-up boots against its side. She sucks in her cheeks and widens her emerald-colored eyes; lines as sharp as arrows form down her face. She purses her lips and poses with her sea-foam green Cover Girl compact. I stand behind a line of young girls, *young women,* rise to my tiptoes and analyze every inch of my face in the mirrors.

"Lipstick?" Kelsey asks and slides down the radiator, her long, stubble-free vanilla legs pouring from a tattered second-hand kilt. I fumble through my purse, an Indian-print satchel held together by safety pins, and toss her a black tube of matte burgundy lipstick. Kelsey squeezes through the wall of matching twin-sets and powder pastel baby-tees, presses her waist against the lip of a sink, and finger combs her thick red hair into messy buns on the sides of her head. The buns remind me of a plush teddy bear, the way they protrude from her crown in two rounded balls. She slides the red-purple lipstick back and forth until it is caked on her lips in flaky layers, kissing her hand between coats to blot. When finished, she leaves a perfect, thick, movie star kiss on the mirror.

Beside Kelsey stands a petite, blue-eyed blonde named Stacy. Stacy's voice is high pitched and her chest flat, but boys love her anyway. At least the good boys do. She and her clan are always clad in neatly-ironed clothing, their arms prepared to shoot to the sky at a moment's notice to answer, with grace and articulation, any question posed by a teacher. To me she is a walking caricature of a Q-tip, with her white-as-snow skin and narrow body, her short bob of fluffy platinum hair. Stacy is so pale that sometimes, while seated next to her in class, I find myself staring at her legs to study the maps of blue veins that trail down her thighs. The translucency of her skin fascinates me.

Stacy adjusts her stiffened collar, smoothes her hair, and smiles at her own reflection in a way that suggests a yearbook photographer is on the opposite side of the looking glass. I lean against a wall, rustle through my bag and begin to flip the pages of a flimsy paperback.

"Hey, Angie," Tina, a preppy girl who lives down the street from me, says. "Heard you did really good on Mr. Williams's test last week. Congrats."

Stacy, who overhears the exchange, briefly looks over one shoulder and eyes me. My cheeks flush as embarrassment settles in.

"No, I didn't," I say.

"Yes, you did," Tina says. "Mr. Williams told me you did. One of the highest grades in the class."

Stacy pushes her thin lips into a straight smile. I try to ignore Tina and keep my eyes focused in the book.

"He's an idiot," I say. "He doesn't know what he's talking about."

"Oh. Well, okay," Tina says. "So, I guess I'll see you at the game this weekend. I think you're playing defense."

My face, I am sure, is the color of cherry ice.

Tina and I play on a soccer team organized by our town. Though a handful of our classmates are in the same league, our team consists mostly of girls from other schools. Many of my friends mock my interest in this sport, including Kelsey, and so I create stories to tell them about how my parents force me to play. Each time my mohawked boyfriend, Jeremy, who I have been dating for several weeks, or a member from our small group of friends takes a stab at me for being a part of the team, I remain quiet. What I do not tell them is that I enjoy being out on the field sprinting beside girls who do not know who I am, or who I try so hard to be. Kelsey, too, often joins in with a sharp laugh. But what she doesn't tell the rest of the group is, every Saturday, like clockwork, she rests on the sidelines of the town field, a cigarette balanced between her lips, and watches me play.

"Yeah, whatever," I say to Tina. I am embarrassed she has just outed the teenage normalcy I work so hard to conceal. I shove my book into my bag, walk inside a stall, and stay there until I hear Tina's light footsteps tap towards the door and into the hall.

Stacy leans against a sink; she watches Kelsey reapply the dark stain to her already reddened lips.

"That's a little dark, don't you think?" Stacy says and raises a brow while her eyes follow the movements of the tube.

Kelsey twists and caps the lipstick and seductively puckers her lips. She throws the tube up and over Stacy's head as I exit the stall; I reach for it, but am clumsy, and so it rattles across the sink. Kelsey sucks her tongue across her teeth.

"You're a little boring, don't you think?" she says without flinching a muscle in her face.

Stacy's jaw drops and for an instant she is left speechless. She shakes her head as though to wake herself from a daydream. In the corner of the room a group of younger girls giggle. They cover their mouths with cupped hands as their hushed laughter becomes louder. Stacy's head twists in one swift motion.

"May I ask what all of you are laughing about?"

As though on cue, the girls' laughter ceases, and, one by one, they begin to file out the door.

Her lids already dark with shadow, Kelsey rims her bottom lashes with ebony liner and sings out the lyrics to a song. *Amazing Grace.* I turn to her and smile. Stacy rubs some tinted lip balm across her thin, dollish lips, glances at Kelsey and rolls her eyes.

"Stacy, why the fuck do you care?" Kelsey says and looks at Stacy's reflection.

"Care about what?" Stacy says.

"About what I'm doing. About what I'm putting on my face."

"I don't care about that. I don't care about any of those things. *You* can do whatever you want."

"Then why in the hell do you keep staring at me?" Kelsey says.

Kelsey kicks her schoolbag across the floor and watches it spin in fast circles until it slams against a wall.

"Face it," Kelsey says. "You're fascinated by me, Stacy. You're too dull and you know it, and it scares you."

Kelsey enters a stall and closes its metal door behind her. *Click. Click. Click.* The room fills with the woody scent of tobacco smoke. I pick the lipstick tube from the sink, wipe away the droplets of water, and cover my lips with the wine-colored stain. Stacy stands at the next sink over and taps her white tennis shoe. She coughs, dramatically, and waves her hand across her face.

"That stuff stinks," she says and looks to me, as though for support. I stick the lipstick into my jean pocket and skim my tongue across my teeth. I remain silent.

"I know you did good on that test," Stacy says and leans in close to me.

"So?" I say.

"Then why did you pretend that you didn't?"

"Stacy, why do you care so much about what other people do?"

"I'm just saying, I know you did well on it, that's all."

"Why? What did you get?" I ask.

"That's none of your business," Stacy says and runs her fingers through her wispy bangs.

"Exactly," I say and pause. "It doesn't matter, Stacy. But if it makes you feel any better, I didn't earn *one* of the highest grades in the class. I earned *the* highest grade in all of Mr. Williams' classes."

The hallway bell buzzes once more; its loud, piercing sound seems to vibrate the walls. Stacy stomps towards the door.

"I'm totally telling Mr. Williams that you guys are smoking in here," she says and presses her hand against the door.

As she does this, Kelsey swings open the stall and flicks her cigarette into the toilet behind her. The room is so quiet that I hear the ember sizzle.

"No you won't," Kelsey says and flushes the toilet with her foot.

"Oh yeah?" Stacy says.

"Stacy, you know you don't have it in you to do something like that."

Stacy extends one of her feet into the hall.

"You guys better get to class," she says and then vanishes behind the swinging wooden door.

I press my back against the cool tile wall, slide my body to the floor and begin to pick at the torn black stocking that peeks through the holes in my jeans. The hallways have silenced. The room has emptied. Only Kelsey and I remain.

Kelsey stands at a sink; she fiddles with her hair, wrapping rubber bands here, sticking bobby pins there, and sings out the lyrics to a Motown tune I no longer recall. I close my eyes and listen to the peaks and valleys of her voice as it ricochets through the room; the way it rises and falls makes me think of black girls I've heard on the radio. Kelsey slams down her purse and sits across from me on the floor. When I open my eyes I see Kelsey holds a plastic liter-sized bottle. She grips its neck with a gentle force and delicately slides her fingers across its metallic label.

"Consider this a gift from my 'rents," she says and rolls the bottle to me.

The thick plastic clunks across every groove in the tile. I hold the bottle in my hands and read from the label as though the words themselves are foreign.

*Orange Dream.*

"Are you sure they won't notice?" I ask.

"Trust me," Kelsey says. "No one will notice it's gone."

The safety seal cracks as I twist open the cap. I sip the watered down, creamsicle-colored liquid. Despite the pre-made cocktail's low alcohol percentage, my chest burns to the point that it brings tears to the inner corners of my eyes. The liquor swooshes as the bottle thuds back across the tile. Kelsey grabs the neck and gulps the stuff like a seasoned alcoholic. She wipes her mouth with her sleeve and rolls the bottle back to me.

I take another few swigs before I feel it: the sluggish sensation that creeps from my toes up through my lids. I laugh at this feeling and the sense of maturity it gives me. I laugh about the fact that Kelsey and I are able to pull stunts like this so frequently. We fill Disney-brand children's sippy cups with vodka and orange juice and suck it through the straws before class. I laugh about the fact that our teachers do not recognize what we are up to or simply do not care enough to put a stop to it. I try to share this thought with Kelsey, but become jumbled, and so instead, I laugh at the words that float from my lips in sloppy, slurred waves. And I just keep laughing. I laugh when Kelsey unclips a safety pin and scratches it against her skin until she almost bleeds. I laugh at the half-empty bottle. I laugh at the familiar feeling of booze that beats through my twelve-year old veins. I laugh, hard, as my head smacks the floor.

When I lift my face from the tiles, I see in the mirror that red indentations are spread across my cheeks like branches, and that the near-empty bottle is flat on its side. The bell rings. I plant my hands on the sink and try to balance my body, but it feels like I am floating underwater, like I am swimming through a dream. Kelsey is a few feet from me, her back to the wall, her black military-style boots jutted forward, her face pointed towards a skylight. *Amaaazinggg Graaace.* I rub my eyes, hoping the gesture will wake me, though it only spreads messy smudges of charcoal liner. I blink and let the makeup smear down my skin in drips. My mouth tastes chalky. The light feels harsh, invasive. The floor is cold and refreshing as I allow my body to slip towards it once more.

Kelsey balances herself against the wall as she stuffs the bottle into her school bag. Crumpled sheets of loose leaf float from her bag like giant snowflakes and litter the floor. She kicks her feet through them and we both fall deep into laughter. In seconds, Kelsey is on her knees amongst the artificial snow. She crawls and dips her head over the ceramic edge of a toilet seat while her bag lays spread open and spewing its contents beside her. I pull myself from the tiles, pat the back of Kelsey's head, stumble towards a mirror and catch a glimpse of my face. For the first time since meeting Kelsey in the bathroom this morning, I am afraid.

"We have to get out of here," I whisper.

Kelsey stands and glances at her reflection. Like a child, she gathers a pile of the paper snow in her arms and throws it above her head. She dances beneath the fluttering flakes.

"We have to go," I say.

Kelsey takes hold of my hand and slips her fingers between mine. Together, we move into the hallway and mix into the sea of students that seem to drift past in a slow motion parade. Our bodies weightless, we glide through the crowd, bouncing off shoulders and walls. She laughs and it sounds like music to me. Our fingers still interlaced, she guides me past a row of faculty, out a set of side doors, across the courtyard, and into a nearby cornfield, into which, together, we seem to melt and disappear.

People are often surprised when they hear that many of my childhood memories revolve around husks and the smell of harvest air.

I was a kid when my parents packed our family's belongings and waved so long to our home in Florida to slither back up the coast to New Jersey, where they both were raised. The small Central New Jersey suburb we moved to was the same town where my father had been brought up. The same fields that he ran through, the same streets that guided his way home, would become ingrained in my mind, and so, I suppose, it seemed quaint for a time.

I remember my sister's head and mine bobbled while the car bounced across a rocky, dirt road, and we peered at the strange surroundings through the backseat windows. My sister, who is eight years my senior, pointed to a small wooded area thick with pines. Weeks later, she would walk me through them to collect piles of dried needles and tell me that bears lived there. Big black bears with teeth like razor blades just minutes from our new home. I ached for the familiarity of coconut trees.

The car creaked to a halt and my parents buzzed down the windows.

"Welcome home," they said and stepped from the car.

Staring back at us was a short row of identical cream-colored homes surrounded by thick fields of corn.

The truth is that the town was meant only to be a transitory stop for our family. My father planned to temporarily take over a family member's small business, which was located just a few minutes from our new home, before we packed back up and moved on to a different part of the state. The temporary plan ultimately lasted the length of my childhood. My mother, who was always anxious for our family to continue heading north, frequently made a point to remind me that our town was not the end of the road for me — that there was an entire world filled with beauty for me to see. And so, perhaps without fully

25

intending to, she bred an escapist's attitude within me. I rarely allowed myself to become attached to the town or its people because, in the back of my mind, I always knew that, one day, I would leave.

As I grew older, every autumn, my father snuck me off to help him cut down stalks of Indian corn. As we hacked through the fields that still towered above my head, my father told me stories of his youth. Stories of finding his way home through the mazes of growth. Of kissing his first love with the whisper of husks upon his back.

The autumn we drove past the fields and found them naked, only row upon row of studded brown stems, I asked my father when the new corn would arrive.

"No corn this year," he said and looked back at the bare plots through the rearview. "The world is changing," he said. And I knew that he was right.

In time, the fields would become foundations for new crops of modular homes.

Kelsey and I met in kindergarten. I remember secretly watching her from across the classroom and being fascinated by her strangeness: I had never seen anyone with red hair. The sight of it both intrigued and frightened me. From my childish perspective the redness reminded me of fire, as though licks of crimson flames coiled down her back.

As our friendship developed, though we had other friends, there was always an undeniable connection between us. A strange type of intimacy or even an attraction of sorts. When I was young, I assumed that connection spawned from similar tastes in generic things, such as music, though now, I understand it was something much deeper. Since childhood, Kelsey shared my escapist desires, and was always looking for a place to run. The only difference between us, really, was that I ran from external forces, things I was guaranteed to escape so long as I tried. Our town. Our bad decisions. Kelsey, on the other hand, ran from forces within her, forces that would grow and strengthen and eventually consume her. Forces she never had a fair chance of escaping.

As teenagers, Kelsey and I often took long drives down roads where houses had not yet been built. The tires spun down two-lane stretches of pavement, the flat road lying ahead like twisting strips of black ribbon. I remember those nights, my head hanging out the car window, my lips chapping from the wind. How I'd studied the moon and its blue reflection washing across the fields like waves. I was fascinated by the idea that, no matter which roads we drove down, the moon always hung just overhead. It reminded me of the type of prop one might see hung above the stage of a small-time production. No matter the scene below it, a giant white cutout that always dangled from the rafters to define an imaginary sky.

I squinted out the window and looked for a string.

So many nights of my youth were spent that way. Kelsey seated to my left, her fingers curled around the wheel. My head pressed against the window frame while the air whipped my hair and dried out my eyes. My gaze fixed on the moon above me while the quiet symphony of husks lulled the world to rest. And I, intoxicated by the midnight light, caught in a belief that Kelsey and I would stay that way, together on an endless drive away from that place, forever and ever.

If I were God, I would revise the script; edit out the Act of Adolescence altogether.

I hated a lot of things back then. I distinctly recall looking down on my peers, certain that I would achieve more than they, perhaps because, by age thirteen, I had already convinced myself that I would leave the confines of our small town and that they never would. I wasted much of my childhood being angry about the way others might choose to live their lives and being scared when I thought about the possibility that their choices might eventually influence me.

But it wasn't just my peers that I hated. I remember that I hated myself a lot back then, too. Terrified that I might not be strong enough to leave that town and thus might never accomplish my many dreams. Convinced I'd never be bright enough to get the grades that would help me escape. Always obsessed with my body. Constantly consumed by the thought of my appearance, or the appearance I desperately wished for. So many hours wasted in front of mirrors to analyze my pores, my belly, my profile, all my new hairs and curves. Somewhere during that time I suffered a growth spurt and woke one morning to find my ankles poking from the cuffs of my jeans. I looked like a stranger even to myself. And so, I began to place blame where blame was due: I turned my obsessive nature towards my legs, too long for their own good, and, subsequently, my arms.

Kelsey stabs a shiny key against the post of a wooden dugout, chipping away at her initials, K.E.F. The sun swelters with the promise of an early spring; it warms the aluminum bench, which burns the backs of my thighs. Beads of sweat gather on my forehead. I stretch my arms above my head and remove my long-sleeved shirt. When I do, I take notice of my flesh. For minutes, I stare with disgust at the brunette hairs that line my arms.

I watch Kelsey's pale arms, exposed through a loose-fitted tank. Her small, rounded muscles flex each time she jabs the wood, showing off the ginger freckles and soft wisps of blonde hair that run from her shoulders to her wrists. Self-conscious, I flip my arms over so only their smooth undersides face me.

"I wish my arms looked like yours," I say.

Kelsey shoves the key into a pocket of her denim cutoffs, yanks a few strings that dangle from the torn hems and takes a seat beside me. Without asking, she lifts one of my arms in her hands; she rests it beside her own and shifts her eyes as she compares the two.

"Yeah," she says, without hesitation. "I probably would too if I were you."

She drops my arm, grins, and kicks her legs in front of her to rest her feet on a wooden beam.

I twirl the tip of my sneaker in the dirt and create a tiny sand storm around my ankles. Kelsey slaps me hard across the back.

"I'm kidding," she says. "You've got to learn how to be less sensitive."

Kelsey playfully tousles the brunette hair that reaches down my back, unzips her schoolbag and tears a sheet of loose-leaf from a notebook. She carries it with her to the center of the baseball diamond, sparks a corner of it with a match, and studies the faint bluish flames that spread across it. I remain quiet, lower my head, and stare at my arms. From the corner of my eye, I watch Kelsey flip the sheet and lift her free hand to her forehead to block the sun.

"If you don't like them, why don't you just shave them?" she says and lets the paper fly from her hand.

But I don't have the guts to verbally confront the fact that I've never even shaved my legs or held a razor in my hands, and that, therefore, the idea never crossed my mind. I don't have the guts to admit that I fear what my mother would say, what other students would say, what *she* would say.

In silence, we watch the flaming paper flicker in the breeze before it singes to ash in the outfield.

Kelsey moves towards me. She reaches into her pocket and pulls out the key. Without speaking, she begins to stab its pointed end into the wood.

"I know you're scared," she says softly. "I know you're scared of what everyone will think."

She turns to face me, leans her back against the wall, and looks towards the outfield.

"You've got to stop worrying about making other people happy. In a few years, half of them won't matter. Half of them won't even remember your name."

Tightness builds in my chest. I try to convince myself it is because I am offended, though, in my heart, I know it is because she is right.

"If you shaved them, would you be happy?" she says, and I nod, my eyes still focused on the ashy dirt.

"Would you feel better about yourself?" she asks.

"I think so," I admit.

"Then I'll do it with you," she says. "We'll skip school tomorrow and I'll do it with you."

Before I have the chance to express my gratitude she turns away from me and resumes splintering the wood.

In the morning, I rise early and quietly jog across my bedroom carpet in an attempt to flush my face. The moment sweat begins to bead along my hairline I climb back beneath the sheets and wait for my mother to come wake me.

When she approaches my bed I flutter my eyelids, as though she has just disturbed me from a long, peaceful sleep. She leans close to my face, and I begin to groan and wheeze. She presses the soft underside of her wrist to my forehead, smoothes back dampened strands of my hair, and whispers into my ear.

"I'll call school to let them know you won't be in today," she says, kisses my cheek, and pulls my blanket further up my chest.

Minutes later, the front door swings shut. I jump from my bed, sprint down the hall, and crouch at the large bay window that faces our drive. Through white, lace curtains I watch as my sister hops into her car and speeds off to her first real job. My mother waits until my sister safely pulls away and then steps inside her own car. I continue to stare through the window until both my parents' cars roll backwards onto the street. When they disappear into the distance I dial Kelsey, humming the familiar tune of the keypad as I press each number key.

"We still on?" I say.

"Oh yeah. My parents and my sister are already gone for the day. I've got my little army all lined up in the bathroom. My razor, shaving cream, bunch of lotions all waiting on the front line," she says.

"Can I ask you a question?" I ask.

"Don't tell me you don't have a God-damned razor or something," she says.

"No. I'm sure my mom or my sister does. I just. Well. I mean. It's just that — "

"Well, what is it? The tub is filling up, so — "

"I just wanted to say thanks. You know, for doing this with me."

"Oh, Christ," she says and sighs dramatically into the phone. "You get so emotional about everything. Look, it's *nothing*, okay?"

"Oh," I say. "Okay."

Before I rest the phone back in its cradle, Kelsey whispers through the line.

"Hey. You're welcome," she says softly and then quickly hangs up the phone.

The tub overflows with a muddy mixture of bath salts and gels, herbal-scented bubbles that cloud the water, and several petals snipped from a kitchen arrangement strictly for effect. The pink, disposable razor feels awkward in my hands as I clumsily rake it through sloppy layers of dripping foam. My skin looks as though it is covered in melting whipped cream. I run the razor across my arms in awkward horizontal, vertical and diagonal strokes until brown spots of blood begin to appear all across the layers of white — the unbearable sting of foam meeting virgin skin. I hold my arms beneath the cloudy water, my torn flesh burning as I watch the foam drift from my skin and evaporate. Clumps of hair float to the surface like schools of dead fish. I lift my arms from the water and watch as thin streams of red spread down them. I cup a puddle of water in my palm and pour it across my skin; it beads and rolls off my arm with grace. The sight of it excites me. For the first time in my young life, I look at my own body and feel beautiful. I feel like a woman.

The next morning, I slip into the most racy thing I own: a striped cotton polo with tiny cap sleeves and black trim. When I arrive at school, Kelsey and a small group of our friends loiter in the bus loop, a cloud of smoke hovering above their heads. She stands beside my boyfriend, Jeremy, who she admittedly has a crush on, and talks to him about obscure punk bands they both adore but I only pretend to enjoy. On most mornings, I would be frustrated with Kelsey for openly flirting with my boyfriend, despite the fact that I have no real feelings for him other than gratefulness for being the first boy to ever ask me out. This morning, though, I strut towards them filled with pride as I rock my hips and swing my smooth, hairless arms in wide, dramatic strokes. But as I near Kelsey, and see that she wears a long-sleeved flannel shirt, I feel like a fool.

"You didn't do it?" I say, lower my eyes, and position my arms behind my back.

"Of course I did it," she says and casually pulls a drag from her smoke.

She flicks her filter onto the blacktop, wraps her fingers around my bicep, and examines my exposed arm.

"Looks *orgasmic*," she says and runs her hands across my newly shaved skin. Her fingers glide up my forearm toward my elbow and accidentally skim a small, pinkish nick. The touch of her fingers makes the nick burn, and, instinctively, I pull away.

"What happened?" she says. "Did you cut yourself or something?"

I shake my head and reach into my bag for a smoke. The menthol flavor burns my throat and I cough the puff out almost immediately.

"You've got to learn to inhale," Kelsey says, momentarily forgetting the few small accidental scabs on my arms. She takes the cigarette from my fingers and lets it dangle between her lips the way old women and truck drivers sometimes do. As she speaks, small flakes of ash float from near her lips.

"It was just an accident," I say. "I wasn't really sure how to hold the razor and it kept slipping out of my hands."

"Well, if it makes you feel any better, I cut myself, too," she says and begins to cuff her shirtsleeves.

As Kelsey slowly reveals her skin to me, I see that, spread across both her arms, scattered throughout the mazes of freckles, are a series of short, thin slashes of scab.

"What did you do?" I say, observing the near dozen cuts that cover each of her arms.

Kelsey explains that her razor became clogged mid-shave. She explains that she tried to clean the blade by swishing it through the water, though the grime did not let loose. In an effort to remove the strawberry blonde hairs that clogged it, Kelsey dug her fingernail beneath the plastic frame. When she did, rather then pick out the mess of foam, she picked out one of the shiny, silvery razors instead. The quick movement sliced the pad of her finger, almost in a seductive way, she tells me. It cut her in a way that left no trace of pain. And so, she slid the razor through her skin again.

And again.

"I mean, it didn't hurt or anything," she says while examining the few scabs on my arms. "That's what was weird. You would think it would have hurt. But I hardly felt a thing."

She pauses briefly, as though waiting for me to offer a response. I say nothing.

"In a weird way, it almost felt sort-of good," she says in what seems an effort to prompt me.

But still, I remain silent. My eyes are fixed on the scabbed designs that cover her flesh. As I study them, I am unsure which bothers me more: the fact that Kelsey took the time to carve through her skin, or the fact that I didn't have the courage or the desire to do so myself.

"Well, whatever. I think they look cool," she says, drops my arm, and begins to roll down her sleeves.

Several days from now, I strive to be like Kelsey. In the shower, I peruse my sister's inventory of mature bath products: vanilla-scented bath gel from a lingerie store, expensive deep conditioning treatments she purchases with the money earned at her first real job. I spot her pink disposable razor at rest beside the bottle of children's detangling shampoo my mother still purchases for me. Once I pick apart the disposable blade, I slowly slice my boyfriend's initials, J.A.T., across the thin underside of my forearm, flinching each time the razor makes contact with my skin. When I step into the hall, partially proud and partially in pain, my mother's eyes immediately dart directly to the marks; she erupts with tears of fear and rage.

"What did you do to yourself?" she explodes. "Are you trying to kill yourself?"

I slap my hand over the cuts to conceal them, suddenly embarrassed by the stupidity of my actions.

"What the fuck are you thinking about? I didn't raise you like this. Who told you to do this?" she screams while sprinting after me down the hall.

A wet towel still wrapped around my head, I run from my house to the nearby dugout where, for hours, I hide and wonder why the touch of the blade did not leave me with the same sense of satisfaction that it did my friend.

When I return home that evening, my mother knocks on my bedroom door and then appears holding a first aid kit. She guides me to the bathroom where she gently pours capfuls of peroxide across each cut on my skin.

"Did Kelsey cut herself, Angela?" my mother asks. She is straightforward, though her tone is much kinder than it was hours ago.

I nod and stare at the white bubbles that ooze from my cuts.

"Did she cut initials, like you did, or did her cuts look like something else?"

"She doesn't have a boyfriend," I say. "Whose initials would she use?"

"It's not about having a boyfriend. I need to know if her cuts look different from yours."

I shrug.

"I don't know," I say, even though I do.

My mother sighs, contemplating my obvious lie.

"Tell me the truth. Why did you do this?" she says.

"I don't know. It just looked cool," I tell her honestly.

"Were you trying to hurt yourself?" she asks.

"No. Why would I do that?" I say, amazed by what I interpret to be her obvious stupidity. *Why would anyone try to intentionally hurt herself?* "But it hurt a lot when I did it," I admit and look at my inflamed skin.

"Look," my mother says while adhering a final bandage to my arm. "I want you to watch Kelsey. Keep an extra eye on her. If you see her do anything unusual — things your other friends aren't doing — I want you to tell me, okay?"

We are both silent while she begins to tidy up her first aid kit.

"And in the meantime," she says, "I'll be watching out for her, too."

But for now, out of either immaturity, or naivety, or fear, I believe Kelsey. I tell myself that she did this purely because she felt the cuts looked cool. I force myself to believe that the cuts that cover her forearms are strictly an experiment in fashion, and therefore, do not see any reason to investigate *why* she intentionally ran a razor through her skin. Like her dark makeup or her combat boots or her studded leather jewelry, I believe she has done this for the sake of her image, and that is all.

My lips lift into a smile as I take one of Kelsey's arms in my hand. I push up the fabric of her shirt and delicately trace my fingers across the scaly, red scabs.

I glance down at the few small accidental nicks on my own arms.

"Mine didn't really hurt much either," I say, even though they did.

In the coming weeks, long, thin cuts will multiply on Kelsey's arms and slowly spread down to her legs, like a rash or a disease. I will never tell my mother or Kelsey's mother or anyone else.

Instead, I will convince myself that, because of the cuts, she is the coolest girl I know.

A memory comes back to me. Kelsey and I are seated in the backseat of her parents' car. It is summer and we are en route to the shore. I can remember knotted strands of hair whipping across my face. I can remember the warmth of the sun as it beat through the windows and burned the tops of my thighs. Yet, I cannot remember what age we were — ten or twelve, maybe — only that we were very young.

Thinking back on things, I suppose we were always very young, even when we felt we were acting very old.

In silence, we watched the landscape blur past through the window frames:

The farmers' stands, speckled along the roadside, that overflowed with baskets of tomatoes bright as flames.

The wide stretches of cornfields that surrounded the narrow, two-lane road.

The scenes rushed past us, and then, in a flash, were gone.

Kelsey angled her body towards mine and held up her open palms. We lightly tapped our hands against our shoulders and thighs before we smacked them against one another's in a rhythmic *clap, clap, clap.*

*Miss Mary Mack.*

We rested our hands and returned to our original game of peering at the roadside. In the distance, the heated pavement steamed with a gaseous haze, like a parade of summer ghosts. The car raced forward and the blurred figures all disappeared.

*All dressed in black. Black. Black.*

I rested my arms on the window frame, watched the world drift past, and noticed that spread all across the roadside was a dusting of sand, glistening like specks of gold.

All throughout my childhood my family took regular trips to the ocean. Each time we did, my father made a habit to point out to us the moment sand began to appear on the side of the road. *It means we're getting close*, he told us, and then winked at me through the rearview. Coyly, I winked back, satisfied by our secret power for determining when we were nearing the waves.

For an instant, I leaned my face out the window, tilted my head, and felt the sun beat like needles against my skin. I closed my eyes, allowed my hair to blow freely, and pretended I was learning to fly. As I did, my nose tickled from the salt-laced air.

*She climbed so high. High. High.*

I opened my eyes and saw a stretch of bright manicured grass ahead. Kelsey unlocked her seat belt and crawled back towards me. We rested our chins along the edge of the window frame and studied the men who wore visors and checkered shorts and tromped across the neatly clipped lawn. They straightened their postures and practiced bending their knees. As our car neared them, Kelsey and I dropped our jaws and screamed. The men threw their clubs to the ground and pouted like children. We roared with laughter and waved to them as we sped into the distance.

*She reached the sky. Sky. Sky.*

Kelsey slid back to her seat and slapped her hands so hard against mine that my skin stung.

*Miss...*

*Mary...*

*Mack.*

I loosened my wrists and shook my hands to rid them of the burn. As I did, from the corner of my eye, I noticed a field of stunted-looking trees. In silence, Kelsey and I watched the vineyard rush past our squared windows, and the shoddy building that sat adjacent to it. From the building hung a rickety wooden sign that read, *Today's Special Tasting: Blackberry Wine.* The sign slowly rocked forward and back in the humid breeze as though in an attempt to wave us inside.

"One day," Kelsey whispered to me, "when we're old enough, we'll go there and drink until our stomachs feel sick."

I nodded, my eyes still fixed on the passing building and fields.

"One day," I said.

*And she never came back.*

37

It is around the time when the air has begun to cool and crisp, has begun to lose the final fragrances of summer. The school buzzer sounds to signal the end of another day. Kelsey and I meet across the street from the schoolyard, a spot just far enough that we can't get busted for smoking on school grounds, but close enough that everyone still sees us puff out little clouds of gray.

We walk through the back streets of our town, tiny streets with even tinier sounding names. Somewhere between Mallory Way and Magnolia Lane, Kelsey tosses her cigarette stub onto the concrete.

"My mom fell down the steps again last night," Kelsey says. She walks along the curb as though it is a balance beam; her body rocks with every step as she tries not to tumble and fall.

"When did it happen?" I say. "I mean, was she — "

"Of course she was," Kelsey says, absently. "Anytime it is after seven-thirty in my house, you can assume that yes, both my parents are drunk."

I have listened to Kelsey tell stories like this before, about her parents' drinking and slurring and stumbling and forgetting. About the cartons of strawberry wine on the top shelf of the fridge; the plastic bottle of vodka that is forever being replaced in the kitchen cabinet; the cases of cheap Genesee beer that stack high in the laundry room on Friday nights and are always gone by Sunday afternoons; about the liquor cabinet in the den that is home to an army of bottles; the menthol cough drops her mother sucks to hide the smell; her father's normalcy in the daytime and rage when the clock strikes eight and his belly is full of tonic and gin. So many years I have listened to these stories. So many times I have sat back and watched new ones unfold.

Kelsey kicks her foot against the curb and refuses to face me.

"Has your mom ever done anything like that?" she asks the ground.

"No," I say truthfully. And then: "I'm sorry."

The full truth, however, is that since becoming parents neither my mother nor my father smoke or drink or do anything borderline exciting or dangerous, which, at times, I resent. Yet, I know Kelsey values this trait about them. The only alcohol that is kept in our home is a lonely bottle of Bailey's that has sat, untouched, in the door of our refrigerator for most of my life.

We turn onto Kelsey's street, a wide stretch of suburban road lined with split-level homes and neatly trimmed hedges. Not too far in the future from now, Kelsey and I will walk, on a day just like this, and find one of her neighbor's homes wrapped with yellow police tape. Officers will wave and tip their hats. Nothing to see here. When we click on the news we will learn that, just past the sunshine-colored strips is the body of a woman bludgeoned to death.

Later, we will hear rumors that, upon further police investigation, Nazi paraphernalia was discovered at the crime scene. From Kelsey's darkened bedroom, she and I will slip our fingers between the slats of window shades and stare with curiosity at the house just down the road. It will fascinate us that something like *that* could happen someplace like *this*.

That something like that could happen someplace like home.

About a block from Kelsey's house is an elementary school; it is the same school she and I attended just a few years ago. We walk to the back of the u-shaped building, across the playground and wide lawn, and self-consciously watch our reflections as they move from window to window. A group of high school girls lead an after-school program. They blow whistles and try to look professional in pleated khakis and oxford shirts. They watch us as we cross to the far side of the lot.

Kelsey and I stop at a waist-high brick wall just outside the school's boiler room. We stop here almost daily, lay our bodies across the scratchy surface and stare at the nothingness in the sky. Kelsey strikes a match against the pavement and lights us each a smoke.

Behind us, a metal door creaks open. Kelsey and I toss our cigarettes to the ground and grind them out beneath our shoes. A man in a green jumpsuit steps onto the concrete. He wheels an industrial-sized garbage can out behind him, leans against the building and lets out a slow sigh; his breath sounds like the hiss of a punctured balloon. For several minutes, the man looks out ahead of him, blankly. I wonder what thoughts go through his head. When he finally turns and observes us watching him, he clutches the can and turns back towards the building.

"You kids better not be smoking or anything out here," he says, emotionless, and then disappears behind the slate-colored door.

Kelsey shuffles through her bag, a cloth satchel adorned with mismatched pins and patches, and fishes out a book of matches from a local pizzeria, the restaurant's logo stamped on its cover in red ink.

"Those were the last of the good ones," she says and looks at the flattened filters on the ground. She hands me a fresh cigarette. "I took these from my parents' carton last night. They're generics. *Dorals.* I swear to God they taste like smoked fucking pork," she says and inhales.

Kelsey tucks her knees into her chest, making her legs form a perfect triangle. In the sunlight, her fiery hair glistens, the color reminiscent of a mixture between straw and rubies. I admire it with wonder. Her cigarette dangles from the edge of her lips. I watch a pale stream of smoke escape her mouth just before she sucks it back up through her nose. This is Kelsey's signature move, a trick she calls a French inhale. She rests her cheek upon her knee, trickles her fingers across her ivory skin and pushes her calf, watching as her flesh swings from side to side.

"Do your legs jiggle that way, too?" she asks, and squints from the trail of smoke that floats towards her eyes.

I lift my legs to mimic her triangular shape and rock my calves from left to right. Neither of us has a pound on our young bodies to spare, and yet we both become transfixed and disgusted by the heavy movements of our skin.

Kelsey lets her legs fall against the side of the wall. She picks at her fingernails.

"Can I ask you something?" she says and flicks her glowing filter to the ground. "What do you think you'll do one day, when we're older?"

I think about it and tell her I'd like to go to college and study poetry. That I'd like to go to Princeton, someday, and learn to write some poetry of my own. Study Shakespeare with professors in hound's-tooth jackets and thick reading glasses. Wake up in the mornings and sip coffee, wear worn out tennis sneakers and preppy scarves like the all-American girls I've seen in movies. Maybe meet a man and learn how to fall in love.

I stare into the clouds and absorb the fantasy of it all.

"What do you want to do?" I ask.

Kelsey straddles the wall and faces me.

"Artist," she says, matter-of-factly. "Big city, art school, something like that. I want to have an apartment with a fire escape. I want to look out my windows and see neon."

She pauses and I believe she too is caught up in the fantasy.

"But it won't fucking happen," she says. "None of it will. I mean, do you really see yourself ever being that old?"

She picks at a scab on her knee and studies it with great interest, scratching the dry, purplish mark until it bleeds.

"Well, yeah," I say. Don't you?"

"No," she says and wipes a pale streak of blood across the wall. "I just don't think I'll ever live to be older than eighteen."

"Of course you will," I say.

And then, without thinking twice about it, I allow these fateful words to slip from my lips: "Only sick people die that young."

"Okay," she says. "Then promise me that it will happen. Promise me that one day, I'll make it to New York. That we'll make it there together. And that every night we'll sit up on our roof and smoke butts and look out at the buildings and see neon."

We intertwine our pinkies and kiss the sides of our hands. The deal has officially been sealed.

"I promise you," I say. "One day, we'll make it there."

Our eighth grade reading teacher, Mr. Smith, stands at the front of the room and clumsily scribbles half-legible notes across the blackboard. His clothes, despite his best efforts, always look cheap to me, like leftovers from a yard sale or clearance rack. I imagine he is the type of man who goes home and dines on frozen T.V. dinners, carefully slicing through his Salisbury steak and pre-made cranberry compote. He pauses, lost in a thought, and adjusts his thick, square glasses. As he resumes writing, yellow chalk dust smears across his polyester sleeve.

Kelsey flicks her eraser against my back and tosses a folded paper triangle onto the corner of my desk. My name is artfully written across it in graffiti style letters.

*My dearest "Thelma,"*

*You doing anything after school? No? Good. Walk home with me! My parents are working late then going to the grocery store, so we can smoke butts inside ... and I can show you their "cabinet." Muahmuahmuah. Write back.*

*Your beloved,*

*"Louise"*

*PS -* Mice and Men *is boring. So very boring. Is the one guy a retard? I don't get it.*

The last period bell rings. Students rush into the halls, open and then slam shut their lockers, and in a breath, are out the door. Kelsey stands beside my locker as I rummage through books and loose assignments. She peeks at her reflection in a small, scratched mirror that hangs inside the door.

"I can meet you at your locker if you want," I say.

"Why would I need to go to my locker?" she asks, still preoccupied with her own reflection.

"Don't you have to bring books home?" I ask.

"I'm not a goody-goody like you," she says and, without asking, shuts my locker for me. "Don't tell me you're actually going to read that book this weekend."

"I liked it," I say while reopening my locker door. "I thought it was touching."

Kelsey kicks back her head in laughter.

"Touching? How old are you? Nobody our age finds books 'touching.'"

"Well I do," I say and gather my final belongings into my bag. "You probably would too if you paid more attention in class instead of acting flirty with all the loser guys who sit around us."

As soon as I open my mouth I feel bad about my words, despite the fact that I mean them. We begin to move through the hallway in silence. Kelsey stays a few feet ahead of me, intentionally pounding her hand against the metal lockers as she walks.

"Hey, I need to stop off in the band room before we leave," she says, apparently forgetting our previous conversation, and finger combs her hair as she drifts down a side hallway. "Got to pick up my clarinet so the perverts don't do anything weird to it over the weekend."

Kelsey spends a great deal of time in the band room, where she begins to learn both her sheet music and the art of seduction. Almost daily, the two male music teachers do all but physically drool at the sight of Kelsey's long, fishnet covered legs, her budding breasts, and her dark rimmed eyes that make her, in their minds, almost a woman. They make lewd comments that in no way relate to an E sharp or C minor, but more to the way Kelsey's young lips press against the instrument's reed. But Kelsey knows how to play their game. She knows the proper way to bat her lashes and slowly cross and then uncross her legs. But perhaps most importantly, Kelsey knows that, despite what the men may think, she holds all the power. One wrong word and she will be in the principal's office, forced tears sliding down her cheeks, with a list of offenses a half-mile long. She knows if she plays her cards right she can score a blank booklet of hall passes from these men each week for the remainder of her middle school career.

By the time we arrive the classroom has already cleared. The two men sit at the center of the room and watch the film, *Amadeus*. Kelsey and I stand near the doorway and peer over the men's shoulders at one of the sexually charged scenes: a giggling Mozart kneels before a woman as he presses his face into her breasts. I nervously fidget with my bag, accidentally slapping it against a metal chair.

"Well," one of the men says and begins to stand. "What are two students doing here so late on a Friday? Detention?"

He raises his lips into a smile.

"Have you two been causing some *trouble?*" he says.

The men look us both up and down, taking us in slowly, and then, in a practiced motion, avert their attention to Kelsey. Their eyes move from her feet, to her nylons, to her black pleather miniskirt, to her round teenage breasts. With their stares, we are no longer in a classroom, but in a smoky bar late in the evening.

"That's a little *racy*," one of the men says.

"You're such a fucking pervert," Kelsey says and rolls her eyes at him.

"Uh, uh, uh. Language alert," he says and shakes his head in disappointment as he momentarily steps back into his teacher role.

"Whatever," Kelsey says. "You don't need to worry. We're not actually here to see either of you. I came to get my clarinet so I can practice over the weekend," she says and disappears into a back storage closet.

The men giggle like schoolgirls, clearly envisioning Kelsey pressing the long, phallic instrument to her mouth.

"So, what about you?" one of the men says and turns to me. "What sort of *racy* things do you have?"

Something in his tone makes me feel dirty, makes a chill run through my body.

"None," I say, tightly wrap my bulky flannel shirt around my torso, and move towards the door.

In the hallway, I watch several straggling students slap each other high-five and tousle one another's hair. I allow my back to slide down the wall until my bottom touches the cool, linoleum floor, and stare at my shoes. I pull the book from my bag — a temporary diversion that allows me to forget about all the things I wish I could flee. The band room door swings open. Kelsey carries her black clarinet box at her side.

"Peace out, creeps," she says and then slams the door shut. She reaches into her bag and pulls out a fresh pad of pink hall passes.

"Did they say anything to you?" I ask her as I bookmark my page.

"Who knows? They're perverts. They totally fantasize about me."

"So why do you go in there? That's creepy."

"No it's not," Kelsey informs me. "It's funny."

"They're your teachers, Kelsey. Why do you even talk to them?"

"I don't know," Kelsey says. "I just do. It's fun for me, okay?"

"It's gross," I whisper.

I stand up, stuff my book into my bag and briefly contemplate why Kelsey's budding sexuality bothers me so much. Perhaps it is because I am still too shy and too uncomfortable with myself to even consider the thought of my own sexuality. I feel bad for a moment and consider apologizing to Kelsey. But by the time I lift my head, her hand is already whooshing through the air. Her open palm smacks my face before I have a chance to realize what is happening.

"If I had a boyfriend, I'd know what to do with him. You dated Jeremy for a month and never did more than kiss him. You barely even hung out with him outside of school. No wonder he dates high school girls now."

But I barely process what she says. I press my hand to my cheek, which still burns from her impact. In this moment I begin to realize that it is not so much Kelsey's sexuality that bothers me; rather, it is the fact that this is the first time I can sense our lives and our interests drifting apart.

Kelsey walks towards the exit of the school and, without thinking twice, I follow her out the door.

We walk several blocks in silence to a corner deli just down the road, a place known for great roast beef sandwiches, potato chips, and selling cigarettes to minors. A small bell jingles to announce our arrival. I wander through the aisles while Kelsey goes straight to the front counter. She leans across it, smiles and bats her lashes at the middle-aged male clerk.

"Cold out there today, huh?" Kelsey says and pretends to shiver.

The man agrees while his eyes remain glued to the content of his newspaper.

"Leaves are really starting to change," she says.

The clerk nods, uninterested, from behind his sports page.

"So, uh, can I get two packs of Marlboro Lights, please?" Kelsey says.

The man lowers his paper and raises a brow.

"You girls look a little young to be smoking, no?" he says.

Kelsey drops her jaw and dramatically widens the size of her eyes.

"Of course we are, sir," she says. "You've got it all wrong. You see, they're for our mom. She's really sick and can't leave the house. She made us promise to stop and pick them up for her on our way home from school."

He squints and remains quiet for a moment.

"Come on," he says. "I've heard that crap before."

"Look," Kelsey says. "I think smoking is disgusting. Personally, I wish my mom would quit, but she's stubborn that way. I mean, I can't tell you why she keeps at it."

Kelsey droops her eyes and rests her elbows on the counter. She lowers her voice to a near whisper.

"But what I can tell you is that if we show up at home without her cigarettes, well, I just, I don't know what she's liable to do."

"Alright, that's enough. Now, you're sure these are for your mom?" he says and cranes his neck towards the door. Kelsey nods. The man reaches his hand into a cigarette display above his head and pulls down two packs. Kelsey spills a handful of quarters onto the counter.

"Sorry," she says. "Mom hasn't been working much since she's been, you know, *ill*."

She grabs the packs and together, we move back into the crisp, autumn air.

"Hey kids," the man shouts through the closing glass door. "Tell your mom to get better. And that she shouldn't be smoking those cancer sticks, either."

Kelsey turns, politely waves to him, and then begins to smack one of the packs, hard, against the heel of her palm. She tosses the pack to me and watches as I unwrap its plastic wrapper, slide a cigarette from the package and press it between my lips.

"A little flirting didn't seem to bother you that time, did it?" she says and lights a cigarette of her own.

We stare blankly at one another for seconds before breaking into a fit of nervous laughter. Kelsey examines my face while a cloud of smoke drifts from her mouth.

"You want to come over?" she asks and I anxiously nod. Kelsey tucks the cigarettes into her bag and wraps her arm around my waist as we begin to move down the street.

In Kelsey's kitchen I kick my feet onto a wooden chair, tilt my head and study the whirling blades of the ceiling fan. I allow thin, silvery streams of smoke to drift from my lips. With each turn of the blades, the soft grayness of the clouds disappears into nothing.

Kelsey lifts herself onto the counter, strikes a match and takes a drag. She shapes her mouth into a circle and puffs out a series of smoke rings. The transparent shapes float through the air, growing in size until they begin to fade to blue and evaporate. Kelsey taps her cigarette against the edge of the sink. A rod of gray ash falls and hisses as it cools. She pushes her bottom from the countertop and begins to scoop heaping spoonfuls of powdered iced tea mix into glasses. On the top of each glass floats a layer of brown, sugary foam. Kelsey takes a sip, licks the foam from her lips, and smacks her mouth, satisfied with her artificial concoction.

We carry our glasses to the downstairs den and pass through the upstairs living room where Kelsey's sister, Erin, and a group of her friends, a combination of preppy high school girls and shaggy haired boys whose faces Kelsey and I have committed to memory, watch MTV and puff away on their own cigarettes. Erin is three years older than us, and Kelsey and I both adore her. She is everything we want to be: intelligent, pretty, artistic, popular. She talks often about colleges and her excitement to graduate high school so that she can leave our town and start life someplace new. I listen to her and fantasize about the classes and books that will soon become a part of her daily life. Kelsey listens and, I believe, fantasizes about the idea of leaving her home for any place new at all.

Downstairs, I settle into a plush, blue armchair. Kelsey rests her drink on a wooden end table, crawls across a sofa and peeks through the slats of the window shades for any familiar cars that may be approaching. The street is empty. For now, her parents remain at their modest office jobs, leaving us with authority over the contents of their den. Kelsey moves to the front of the room and swings her arms in a wide swoop towards a shuttered door built into the wall.

"You ready?" she says.

I roll my tongue to mimic a drum roll and slap my hands against my knees.

Light illuminates the slivers in the wood as Kelsey begins to slide open the doors. The lights flicker and then fully spring to life. Rows of bottles are lined up like hostages who have waited for us to come free them after all this time. I move closer, amazed by the assortment, bottles in shapes and colors I have never seen — green and brown and pink, thick-necked, no-necked — all staring back at us, as though they too have anxiously anticipated this moment. On the back wall is a mirror in which ingredient labels become aligned with Kelsey's reflection and mine.

"I don't know what half of them are, except that they all burn like hell," Kelsey says and reaches for an electric green bottle of watermelon schnapps. "I don't think anyone will notice if we take this one. My parents only really bother with these," she says and points to plastic liters of vodka and gin.

"What about Erin?" I say. "Is she going to say anything?"

"Erin?" Kelsey says through a laugh. "She has been doing the same thing with her friends for years."

Kelsey and I take turns sipping from the bottle. The liquid is fruity, yet spicy, like a lollipop with a cayenne kick. We swig from the bottle. The more sips we take, the more the burn seems to fade. We gulp from the bottle. Before we know it, almost half its contents are gone. For no good reason, Kelsey and I are overtaken by laughter and begin to wrestle, playfully pushing one another to the ground. We spill the mutant-colored liquid across the carpeting. Our laughter echoes. Erin and her friends enter the den. The boys, whose attention Kelsey and I practically beg for by way of our immature giggling, give us a once over and then blatantly mock us for being too young to know how to handle our booze. Erin observes us and releases a sigh.

"Jesus Christ, Kelsey," Erin says. "If you're going to do this you better get out of here before mom gets home."

Kelsey slides an end table a few inches forward to cover the setting stain. Although Erin is guilty of many of the same things as Kelsey and I, she never encourages her younger sister to drink or to smoke or to do anything that might harm her.

"I have to go to work," Erin says. She sets down her book bag and searches inside it for the black apron she wears at her part-time job. "If mom comes home and sees you like this," she says, "I never saw you. I don't feel like having to deal with her wrath when I get home."

Kelsey looks to Erin and acknowledges her comment. Erin closes the door behind her. Kelsey readjusts the table one last time. It will remain in this position, unnoticed, for several years.

Kelsey clumsily runs towards her bedroom. Her body slams against the wall with every step she takes. My face pressed against the floor, I begin to move my arms and legs and pretend to make snow angels on the carpeting on a crisp autumn afternoon.

The magical nature of booze.

When Kelsey returns, she crawls beside the entertainment center and throws a CD towards it, like a Frisbee, before she realizes she must clutch onto the cabinets, lift her body back up and drop the CD into the electronic tray. Music shakes through the speakers and trembles a row of picture frames. Inside the liquor cabinet, bottles ting against one another. Kelsey pulls me from the floor. We jump across the couch, slap each other with the cushions, laugh and sing until we both fall down.

Back upstairs, in the bathroom, I sit along the edge of the tub and watch Kelsey as she rummages through cabinets and drawers. She pulls out bottles of her mother's creams, fumbles through boxes of cotton balls, and throws handfuls of tampons to the sky. We squeeze Skin-

So-Soft-scented lotion across our skin and press flesh-colored powder against the tips of our noses. Kelsey uncaps a black eye pencil and reads the fancy name written across its side in delicate gold. *Estée.* We pass the pencil back and forth, pull down our bottom lashes, and run it across the narrow line of sensitive flesh. Broken, black chips float into my eye and force several tears down my cheeks. When the pencil is worn to a nub, we examine our reflections, satisfied with the image of makeup on our faces and the scent of liquor on our breath.

My body is gracelessly spread across the floor of Kelsey's bedroom when we are both awakened by the invasive sound of a car horn. I pull my body up, wipe at my eyes and splash myself with a mist of juniper body spray. The ground beneath me seems to shift like a funhouse floor.

Outside, the sky has turned to black. Up and down the road, yellow street lamps flicker. I swing open the car door and try to act normal. The interior light shines across my face like a ruthless detective's lamp. Before my mother even opens her mouth to speak, I know I am caught.

"Wash that shit off your face when we get home," she says and begins to back the car from the drive.

Even though my vision is blurred, I can see my mother's disappointment and the look of sadness in her eyes. Despite my smile and jovial greeting, I know she knows. And for this, I feel sadness, too.

"Why are you doing these things?" my mother asks.

"I don't know," I tell her truthfully.

"I don't like the way you girls are influencing each other," she informs me.

"So what? Am I not allowed to hang out with my best friend anymore?"

"That's not what I said at all," my mother says. "That girl needs you far more than you'll ever know."

The car rolls onto the street. The movement makes my head feel much heavier than it ever has. When I look up, I notice Kelsey at her bedroom window. Her mouth is wide with laughter. Two black circles are still stamped around her eyes. In her hand is a glass of half-drunk iced tea.

I wonder if Kelsey, too, will be caught. If, when her parents arrive home, they will notice the adult scent that seeps from her skin. If they will notice her playful sense of ease.

But even through my fogged mind I know what will really take place. Kelsey's sister will stay at a friend's house for the night, leaving Kelsey alone in her bedroom until her mother and her father have become lost, floating in alcoholic seas. Once they have, Kelsey will emerge and sit in the living room beside her mother, who will sip a glass of blush wine. Or she may move into the den to speak with her father, who will be drinking from a sweating glass. It doesn't matter which. What matters is, tonight, there will be no disagreements or slamming doors. For Kelsey, there will be no confusion about her parents' heightened emotions, or heartache over words that they speak, because tonight, she will finally feel the same as they do.

I watch my friend at her bedroom window. She raises her glass to me. As the car moves further down the street, in the rearview, I think I see her mouth forming the word, *Cheers*.

We grew up in the same town. All through our childhood, Kelsey and I walked the same suburban streets; all through our teenage years, we felt the same longing to escape them.

The land around our homes was flat. Every backyard had a swimming pool, most of which were blue, plastic shells set in the center of lawns; only a lucky few had theirs dug into a hole in the ground. Many of the houses were decorated with shiny vinyl siding. Most of the driveways boasted basic American-made cars.

As children, we often see things differently from what they are. In my memory, I imagine greater things were there: fields of dandelions that seemed to stretch on forever; deep woods with weaving paths and streams; large hills that rolled high through my yard.

My family has since moved on from that town, though I've been back as an adult to revisit it, disappointed to see that many of my memories are distorted. The rolling hills were only bumps in the grass; the vast fields a small patch of land; the deep woods consisted of only a few pines. In truth, there were no hills there, no mountains, no people trying to move any either. My childhood was one of middle class-comfort wafting on the scent of over-chlorinated pools.

I often think of the geography of that town. That region of the state is known for its flatness — the same flatness that often gave me the false illusion that the fields of my childhood stretched well past the horizon. But there were many times that I failed to find the sense of flatness intriguing. I recall the year I passed my driving test and the overwhelming sensation that came over me as I drove through the town's streets. No matter which road I turned down, everything before me remained on the same even plane. No roads ever offered a higher elevation, making it seem as though I were trapped among the neighborhoods of identical homes. The thought was suffocating.

The town where I now live, the town where I will raise my

own family, boasts streets that wind up and over high hills and small mountains. Once in a while, in the evenings, before I retire to sleep, I drive my car to the top of my street. I park in a recreation area, sit on the hood and look down at the twinkling lights of my town and at the Manhattan skyline that glimmers in the distance. The sight of neon on the horizon brings me a sense of peace.

When we were in elementary school, Kelsey took horseback riding lessons at a small farm adjacent to our schoolyard. The farm was not large. It spanned only a couple acres of flat land. Though at the time, to us, it seemed enchanted.

The only thing that separated the farm from the schoolyard was a thin wire fence, which should have been repaired, but never was, all overgrown with honeysuckle and buttercups. Many days, during recess, Kelsey walked me to the fence so that we could look out to the farm, to that place that seemed so exotic. We sat in the grass against the fence, Indian-style, while she showed me how to peel back the petals of the honeysuckle and suck on the sweet, hidden drops. We would pluck buttercups and hold them beneath one another's chins to see if they cast a faint, golden glow.

Often, Kelsey and I would peek through the fence and try to see past the layers of braided growth. She would describe the small barn and tell me what it felt like to go rushing down the dirt paths. Sometimes, she told me, on weekend mornings, the owners would let her take one of the smaller ponies outside the fence and into the schoolyard, where they would go galloping past basketball hoops and classroom windows. As a child, listening to those stories, I envisioned Kelsey as a princess, like a character from a fairytale. A cascade of red waves bouncing down her back, an ethereal gown that billowed across her body with the breeze, a circle of buttercups placed delicately on the crown of her head.

Such simple things have the power to seem so magical when you are young.

By the time Kelsey and I were in middle school, the town had begun to break ground to create space for another new neighborhood of identical modular homes. By the time we were in high school, the farm was gone.

As on any morning, Kelsey, several friends and I stand in the bus loop, our eyes still crusted with sleep. The autumn air has begun to grow crisp with the promise of an early winter. We all huddle close to each other to keep warm. I ball my jacket sleeves into my fist and exhale an icy cloud that seems to go on forever. Kelsey hands me a cigarette. I inhale and savor the smoke as it burns through my insides.

Jenny, a student in our grade, approaches us. Jenny is a thick and gawky girl. Her wide legs, broad shoulders and raspy voice, for some reason, remind me of a cartoon giant — a clumsy character from a picture book I once read as a child. I watch Jenny while we are in classes from time to time. Her eyes never focus on the blackboard, but rather, on the flakey stains on her t-shirts. She wipes them with the pink rubber tip of her pencil. Sometimes, I think Jenny wishes she could erase herself.

Jenny's self-consciousness seeps from her skin like a musky perfume. She stands near us, without speaking, allowing instead the spongy filter of her cigarette to occupy her silent lips. I know deep down Jenny only wants to belong. And yet, each time she tries, something happens inside her, like some sort of defense mechanism that suddenly clicks on; her attempt almost always ends in a conflict between her and Kelsey.

Jenny's cigarette burns down and turns to a tube of ash; she lets it slide from her fingers and fall to the ground. She begins to speak. In a matter of minutes, Jenny and Kelsey are shouting in each other's faces. I hardly hear what they say. Exchanges like this are so frequent that I stopped listening months ago. I drop my cigarette and watch it burn beside the curb. When I look up, Jenny's face is blotchy from an explosion of tears. The bell rings and we all scurry inside.

When Kelsey and I receive pink slips during homeroom it is no surprise to step through the door marked, *Guidance*, and find Jenny seated on the far end of the room. Her face is still streaked with pink, her eyes glassy. She lifts her head, looks at Kelsey and me, and then tilts her face back to the floor. Our counselor, Mrs. Walsh, thumbs through a stack of paperwork and shakes her head in disappointment. She finds no need to turn and face us.

The guidance office feels cold. Beige cinder block walls blend into beige, school-issued furniture, which all blends into beige linoleum flooring. It is meant to be a place of inspiration, a personal pep rally complete with smiley face stickers and gold stars. Overhead, florescent lights buzz loudly just before one rod flickers and dies.

Mrs. Walsh's practical heels click against the floor. She pulls a manila folder from a filing cabinet and casually flips through it. *Huh*, she says, in a voice loud enough for Kelsey, Jenny and me to hear. Her desk chair squeaks when it swivels towards us. For a moment, she watches the three of us and does not say a word. She wheels her chair closer to Kelsey, her face stern, serious.

"So. Kelsey," Mrs. Walsh says.

She places her hands on the armrests of her chair and cranes her neck. Tiny wrinkles form between her brows. The scene seems so rehearsed, as though any minute, Mrs. Walsh will pull out her badge, slam down a Styrofoam cup of coffee and shine a lamp across Kelsey's face.

"Would you like to tell me, in your own words, what you said to Jenny this morning?" she says.

To me, Mrs. Walsh is the school's equivalent of a Stepford Wife. She likes students to be neat and tidy and to appear in a certain way. But Kelsey fucks this whole plan up. And so, during our meetings, rather than discuss Jenny's mixed emotions or her constant accusations, Mrs. Walsh uses the time to interrogate Kelsey. She asks her about the boots she wears, and questions if they have anything to do with Nazis or skinheads. *What are your thoughts, by the way, on white supremacy?* Sometimes, Mrs. Walsh questions Kelsey after school pep rallies for having displayed a little too much spirit from the stands. *Have you ever tried pot, cocaine, Ritalin? You can tell me, Kelsey. It's okay.*

Kelsey knows how to play into Mrs. Walsh's games though and offers responses laced with sarcasm. The only time Kelsey did not rely on sarcasm was when she tried to discuss her family. During a private meeting with Mrs. Walsh, Kelsey described her family tree and the disease of alcoholism in almost every branch. She described how she and her sister have dinner at six o'clock each night while their mother sits in the living room, smokes a cigarette and watches reruns of Jeopardy. How at seven-thirty, another meal is served, this one for her parents. This private meal is meant to hide the drunken haze that settles upon them while they slice through their steaks. Yet, almost every night, by nine, the jig is up. One of her parents slams a door or slurs words or stumbles drunkenly across the carpeting. Her mother keeps a notepad on the kitchen counter, her "to-do" list, where she writes all the things she knows she will forget. *Pick up dish soap. Buy more boxed wine. Kelsey grounded for two weeks for calling me a drunk.* Come morning, her mother flips through the notepad and tries to decipher the chicken scratch scribbled across every page. When she screams at Kelsey and reminds her of her punishment, Kelsey rarely accepts it with grace.

"Why am I grounded again? Do you even remember?" Kelsey asks.

Usually, at about this point, her mother throws in the towel, crumples the pages and tosses them in the trash before she heads out the door.

To Mrs. Walsh, this information was a little too serious, and so, very quietly, she decided the game between her and Kelsey was done. By the time Kelsey begins coming to school with slashes on her arms, lines of dried blood so thick I sometimes think you can see them through her sleeves, the game has long been over. There are no rematches, no pink slips, no casual meetings, or detective-style interrogations. Mrs. Walsh never asks Kelsey about her family or her home, or anything that took place outside of the school's boundaries again.

Kelsey and Mrs. Walsh go back and forth, bickering like children.

"I didn't *do* anything," Kelsey says and rolls her eyes.

"Well, you must have done *something* to upset Jenny this morning, otherwise why would she have asked that you be called down here?" Mrs. Walsh says.

Anytime Kelsey opens her mouth, Mrs. Walsh finds a reason to interrupt her and begin a new argument. When Kelsey tries to explain or defend herself, Mrs. Walsh finds a way to shift things and make Kelsey the heart of almost any problem. I know I should speak up, try to defend my friend, tell Mrs. Walsh she is out of line, or nudge her to dig a little deeper, to pinpoint the issues that really boil just beneath Kelsey's surface. But I am afraid I will say the wrong words or add more fuel to their fire. I am afraid of letting myself become too involved. I remain a silent observer instead.

"You think this is all a joke, do you?" Mrs. Walsh says. "You think you can get away with whatever you like?"

"I don't think that at all," Kelsey says.

"Then what do you think? Please, enlighten us," Mrs. Walsh says and leans back in her chair.

"You want to know what I think?" Kelsey says. "I think it is bullshit that you've called me down yet again to talk about some issue that has more to do with Jenny than with me. She's the one who is upset about something. Why don't you make her talk for a while?"

Mrs. Walsh places down her pen and breathes deeply. She glances over at a series of picture frames that are neatly arranged on her desk and takes one in her hand.

"Look at Kerri here," Mrs. Walsh says. Kerri, our classmate and Mrs. Walsh's daughter, has a tiny waist, a big smile, and blonde hair that glistens. "When Kerri gets angry about something, she doesn't smoke cigarettes or curse or scream or wear black makeup. She finds other ways to get out her frustrations. More *healthy* ways," Mrs. Walsh says.

"What makes you think I'm angry?" Kelsey says. "The only thing I'm angry about is that you've pulled me out of class again for this bullshit, and you won't even listen to me."

"You'd better watch your mouth, young lady," Mrs. Walsh says sharply and slams the frame on her desk.

"I also think it is bullshit that I'm being blamed for whatever bug Jenny's got up her ass," Kelsey says in a cool, even tone.

"You're skating on thin ice," Mrs. Walsh says. Her chest and neck flush to a shade of splotchy pink.

"You know what else I think?" Kelsey says and turns to Jenny. "I think that whatever issue you've got, you need to get the fuck over it. In case you couldn't tell, coming down to this office everyday is not helping anyone."

For an instant, Jenny lifts her face from her knees and looks at Kelsey. Somewhere, hidden behind her forceful tone, Kelsey's voice has expressed an ounce of compassion. Jenny recognizes this and smiles.

Kelsey takes a deep breath and resettles herself in her chair. She twirls a strand of hair around her fingertip.

"Why do you have such a problem with me?" she says and looks up at Mrs. Walsh. "If you would just listen to me for once, you'd know I'm not as bad as you make me out to be."

In a very even voice, Mrs. Walsh says the only problem she has is with the fact that Kelsey takes everything as a joke: the way she dresses, her grades, these meetings.

"The fact that I'm the only one in here getting in trouble is a joke," Kelsey says. "Jenny was the one who came down here with a problem this morning. If she has an issue with something I said or did — "

"Maybe the real problem here, Kelsey, is that you were smoking on school grounds again this morning."

"What the hell does that have to do with anything?" Kelsey says and throws up her hands. "Is that why the three of us are down here? Because of a few cigarettes? Everyone was smoking this morning, including Jenny. Smell her fingertips."

"Kelsey," Mrs. Walsh says. "I'm going to have to ask you to calm down."

"I am calm," Kelsey says. "You always do this. Why do you always make me out to be worse than I am?"

Mrs. Walsh crosses her legs and bites the cap of her erasable pen. She indulges in a dramatic pause and allows her eyes to wander across us. She stops and focuses on Kelsey.

"Because I just don't think that you're going anywhere," she says and tilts back in her chair.

Mrs. Walsh turns her gaze to the window and stares towards the trees, searching, perhaps, for a more appropriate, more inspirational response that exists somewhere amongst their limbs. She brushes two silver strands of hair from her face and wheels her chair towards Kelsey.

"Not with an attitude like *that*, anyway," she says.

She smiles, content with her own statement, and crosses both her arms across her chest. End of story. Done deal. The judges have made their final decisions.

Kelsey rests her school bag on her lap and busies herself with its zippers. She pretends not to listen. I watch her chest rise slowly as she breathes. I know that somewhere, past the hurt and frustration of this moment, she has heard, and will always remember.

Mrs. Walsh drums her press-on fingernails across the edge of her desk in a slow, methodic rhythm.

"But, I suppose that none of this matters to you. It's all just part of your act. Part of your 'I don't care about anything' act, isn't it?" she says.

Kelsey lifts her head and presses her lips together so hard that, for a second, I cannot tell if she is going to laugh or cry.

"This is such shit. I don't even know what you're talking about anymore," Kelsey says. She slides the straps of her bag around her shoulders, moves towards the door and touches the knob.

"So," Mrs. Walsh says. "You're just going to get up and leave, *Kelsey*?"

She says her name with such force, it sounds like an obscenity.

Kelsey bites the top of her lip, smearing her dark, purplish lipstick outside the lines of her mouth.

"Thank you, Mrs. Walsh, for all your expertise," she says in a calm and respectful tone. "I really feel like I'm heading in a much more guided direction now."

She slams the door shut, hard, behind her. Its echo fills the silence of the room.

I am unsure if I should leave or stay seated. I scan the walls and notice several posters marked with inspirational words and phrases. *Achieve. Reach for the Stars. Dream.* One of them has a picture of a cat tugging balloon strings.

Jenny looks up at me. "I'm sorry," she whispers and covers her face with a wrinkled tissue.

My focus falls onto the window, to the empty schoolyard, to the piles of burnt-colored leaves that blow gracefully across it. The wheels of Mrs. Walsh's chair scuff across the floor. She sits with her back to us.

"You know," she says. "*You* have a lot of promise. A lot of *po-ten-tial*. I'd hate to see you waste it by hanging out with a girl like — "

"You don't know her," I say, a little louder than intended.

Mrs. Walsh spins her chair back around. She looks surprised to have heard my voice at all.

"You're right," she says, emotionless. "That was wrong of me. I apologize."

She hands Jenny and me each a pink slip.

"You girls better get back to class," she says.


Jenny walks beside me, her shoulders hunched forward, the tip of her nose still raw. Our footsteps echo down the long, empty stretch of hallway. While we walk, I run my hands across the rows of lockers.

Jenny stops and presses her back against the wall.

"So, why does Mrs. Walsh have such a problem with Kelsey, anyway?" she says. She stares at me, waiting for some profound response. I shrug.

"I don't know," I say. "She just always has."

"Do you think Kelsey will get in trouble?" Jenny says. Her voice quivers when she speaks. "I mean, I don't want her to get into any trouble. I don't want anything bad to happen to her, you know? That's not what I meant to happen."

*I just don't think that you're going anywhere.*

"Yeah," I say. "I know you didn't mean it, Jenny."

The bell rings. In a heartbeat, classroom doors swing open and students pour into the hall. I glide my fingers across the cool metal lockers, allowing them to slip carelessly over rows of raised slits.

"I'm not sure what will come out of all this," I say.

Later that week, for the first time, Jenny will approach Kelsey and me and ask, in a straightforward fashion, if we'd like to get together over the weekend. That Saturday, the three of us will spend the afternoon listening to a Pink Floyd album and smoking pot until the world feels okay. In a stoned haze, we will laugh about Mrs. Walsh until our cheeks ache. The three of us will never have a group meeting with her again.

Years later, when I am away studying at college, I will hear a rumor that Mrs. Walsh's daughter, Kerri, has become a casino dancer in Atlantic City. The once clean-cut blonde has chosen to make her living wearing sequins, shaking her breasts and flashing the smile that once made her mother so proud.

I suppose at some point, we all need a way to release the anger we've kept hidden for so long.

Kelsey begins to talk about a boy named Steve. During our eighth grade year, every morning for several months, our friends and I huddle in the bus loop while Kelsey tells us stories about Steve. He picks her up on weeknights, she says, after the whole world has gone to sleep. They cruise through the streets in Steve's car and smoke slow, tightly rolled joints, one right after the next. Steve, who is seventeen, is very impressed by Kelsey, who is just thirteen. He tells her that, by the time she reaches high school, she will be the coolest girl in town.

Kelsey raises her arm, takes a long puff of a cigarette, and tells us in-depth details about her wild nights with Steve. A cloud of smoke escapes her mouth as she describes the way Steve's lips feel when pressed against her neck. She describes the way the pot tastes on her tongue and the burnt smell it leaves on her fingertips. She describes the dusty, gray interior of Steve's car. But what Kelsey never describes is how she and Steve met, what school Steve attended, what street he lives on, or his last name. Rather, she stretches, lets out a long, dramatic yawn, and describes their make-out session that lasted until dawn.

While Kelsey relives her evening rendezvous, I cannot help but to think of my own nightly routine. Flannel pajamas by eight o'clock. Engaged in a family sitcom by nine. Tucked in and dreaming by ten. I pity myself for not having the courage to climb from my bedroom window and down a rope of knotted sheets. For not being brave enough to sneak out the front door of my home in the middle of the night, the way I know Kelsey's sister does, and the way Kelsey claims she now does, too. For not having the guts to ride in a car without my parent's permission. For never kissing a boy beneath the blaze of streetlamps. And so, from time to time, I ask Kelsey if Steve would swing by my place some night.

"I'd like to come along for a ride, too," I say.

But Kelsey looks at me with blank eyes.

"No," she says, flatly. "Steve doesn't like hanging out with anyone but me."

When we are in the ninth grade, the Internet becomes an overnight success and, without warning, homes buzz from the electric glow of clunky computer screens. Every night, Kelsey spends hours staring at the monitor, furiously typing conversations to all her new Internet friends. Her chat room friends. But they are not just computer friends, she tells me. She spends time with these people whenever I am not around. They go to concerts and to the city and to coffee houses. They meet older boys, attend poetry readings and snap their fingers in approval. They frequent consignment boutiques and model hats and sunglasses whose owners are long dead. They do all the things Kelsey and I want to do, but cannot, because we are still too young.

My stomach grows queasy each time I imagine Kelsey being whisked away with these people I've never even seen. *Ryan. Sara. Adam.* Their names ring through my head. I'm jealous each time I listen to stories about Kelsey and her new friends zipping up and down the highway, windows rolled down, hair flapping, while they puff away pack upon pack of cigarettes. I yearn for a secret life of my own. I ache to leave our small town and go on adventures, too. And so, now and again, I ask Kelsey if her new friends would plan an outing on a day I am also free.

"I'd really love to meet them all sometime," I say. "I'd really love to come along, too."

But, according to Kelsey, her new friends tend to be busy on all the days I am not. Mostly, they are from towns I've never heard of.

In high school, I fall into my first real relationship with a boy named Brad. Brad is three years older than me, has dark, kind eyes and makes my heart flutter with the feeling of true teenage love. I begin to spend a great deal of my time with Brad. I sit on the curb of a local parking lot and watch Brad and his friends skateboard across the pavement, cheering each time Brad lands a difficult trick. Afterwards, he takes me out for strawberry milkshakes and holds my hand under the table. We go on dates to the local movie theater. For my birthday, he purchases me concert tickets. For Christmas he gives me my first bottle of Chanel perfume.

It is during this time that Kelsey begins to tell me about a boy named Shane. Shane is from Pennsylvania, has spiky hair, a lip piercing, and a fast car. She keeps a picture of him tucked inside her wallet and now and again looks at it with lover's eyes. I ask Kelsey when I will meet Shane. She opens her wallet and pulls out the creased up magazine clipping, which she explains to be an old shot of Shane's band. If she has a photo of him, I guess, he must be real.

Kelsey tells me she lost her virginity to Shane one weekend when I was out of town, off in Philadelphia with Brad to watch a professional skateboarding competition with him and some of his friends. Kelsey and Shane drove along the highway, hand in hand, she says, over bridges and state boundaries, all the way to his apartment. Once there, they kissed each other softly, tangled up their bodies and crashed onto Shane's bed. They rolled across the mattress and, just as he thrust inside her, a firework display exploded outside the window above their heads. They made love like that, all night, beneath the popping bursts of red and gold.

"It was beautiful," Kelsey says. "Just like a movie."

And I believe her. It does sound beautiful. Still a virgin, I close my eyes and try to imagine someone else's flesh rub against mine. I try to imagine the romance of an illuminated sky.

"But wait," I say. "What were the fireworks for?"

Kelsey hesitates for a moment and then fingers the magazine clipping.

"I don't know," she says. "I guess they were for the Fourth of July."

But it is already early autumn.

"That doesn't make sense," I say. "Fourth of July was weeks ago."

Kelsey looks me in the eye and doesn't say a word. Something in her vacant stare makes the truth of it all finally become evident to me.

Kelsey lies.


Scattered across the sofas and floor of Kelsey's den is a group of our girlfriends, all wrapped under afghans and quilted sleeping bags, playing a game of truth or dare.

"I had my stomach pumped once," Kelsey says and tucks her feet

64

beneath her behind. When she sits like this, her legs remind me of two amputated stubs.

Expressions of shock spread across the faces in the room. Thirteen and fourteen-year-old girls drop their jaws and crane their necks in horrified wonder. I, too, am taken aback. This is not the response any of us had been looking for.

"I was really young, though," Kelsey says and reaches for a handful of potato chips. She smashes them in her fist with a relaxed gesture.

"It was all medicine cabinet-type stuff. Cold remedies, cough syrup, some random pills." She shakes the crushed bits into her mouth. "You know, back when we were still in elementary school," she says.

The room is so still, I hear her grind the chips between her teeth.

Around Kelsey's den, girls survey one another's expressions. There is Carrie, whose blonde, untamed curls make me think of a lion's wild mane. Lindsey, the foulmouthed, 5'2" tomboy. Julie, the olive-skinned, gazelle-like beauty. And Katie, who, despite her best efforts, never seems to fully fit in. But regardless of our teenage awkwardness, or individual insecurities, there are no secrets or strangers in this room. We have all been friends for years. At any given second, we can rattle off one another's favorite colors, favorite foods, or favorite bands. We can recite, in alphabetical order, the names of each other's parents, siblings and pets. For the rest of our lives, our minds will be ingrained with the best shortcuts to each other's childhood homes.

Until Kelsey's statement, there were no skeletons in any of our closets or shameful memories hidden beneath any of our beds. A moment ago, we were the American cliché: teenage girls, a birthday slumber party, and a game of truth or dare. We placed prank phone calls. We gossiped about secret crushes. We pried each other for juicy details about first kisses. But now, with Kelsey's comment, we have become something else: teenagers who marvel at the prospect of child suicide.

Katie slips a blanket further up her chin and inserts a handful of pretzels into her mouth with dazed eyes. She scoots her bottom towards the edge of the couch as though watching a gruesome horror film.

"Why?" she says through a whisper. "Why did you do that?"

Kelsey scoops up another handful of chips and wipes her greasy hands across her thighs.

"Just because," she says coolly. "I don't really know why. I guess I was just bored. I guess I just felt like seeing what would happen."

Through the open window, a gust of late October wind blows across the room. It carries with it the scent of chimneys, the crinkling sound of dried leaves, and gently rocks streamers and party decorations that float from the ceiling. I wrap my sleeves around my fists and examine Kelsey's face. I wait for her to explode with laughter at the practical joke she has just told.

"I was curious," Kelsey says. "You know, to see what all that stuff would really do. You know, to see if it would — "

"I don't buy it," Carrie says and fills her mouth with cheddar tortilla chips. "We would have known about something like that," she says through a crunch. "We all would have heard about that somehow."

With the crisp, nighttime breeze, metallic birthday banners billow above Kelsey's head like a series of unclasped halos. She shrugs her shoulders, tosses a chip into the air, and catches it in her mouth.

"I was a kid. We were all kids. My parents made sure nobody knew," Kelsey says and dips her hand back into the bowl. "But if you don't believe me, just ask my mom. She'll tell you."

For a moment, each of us becomes wrapped in thought, searching through mental archives in the hopes of finding a reminder or a clue. The flash of a memory. The beginnings of a rumor. An image of Kelsey's empty desk chair at school. We scan our minds and hope to determine if what Kelsey has said is true, or just another of her stories.

Kelsey lies.

From across the room, eyes meet, posing questions. Shoulders raise and lips begin to lift into smiles. Julie runs her fingers through her hair and narrows her eyes. She tosses a pillow across the room. It slaps Kelsey's chest.

"You're such an ass," Julie says and tilts her head back in laughter. One by one, we all break into nervous giggles. Without speaking a word, our teenage jury has silently reached a verdict: *Story*. Lindsey slides a CD into the stereo. Carrie passes around a bowl of chips.

"So, who's up next?" Carrie says and drums her fingers.

In just seconds, we return to stories of adolescent love and innocent dares and, amidst the soft sounds of rock music and immature laughter, Kelsey's story, like so many before it, fades away.

The stairs exhale a whiny creak followed by a light shuffle across the hallway floor. Kelsey's mother enters the den, adjusts her eyeglasses and takes a brief survey of the room.

Kelsey's mother appears fragile to me. Years from now, when I think of her and her gangling frame, I will envision the cartoon character Olive Oyl. In the daytime, Kelsey's mother dresses in loose-fitted pleated khakis, practical loafers and cotton turtlenecks; in the evenings, she bundles herself beneath a baggy terrycloth robe. Nearly every day, when school lets out, I walk with Kelsey to her house. We spend hours listening to rock albums and plucking chords on her father's 12-string guitar. Nearly every evening, when Kelsey's mother returns home from work, she hunches over the kitchen sink, releases a long, breathy sigh, mixes herself a cocktail, and smokes a slow cigarette. Kelsey and I sit at the kitchen table, drink glasses of sweetened iced tea, and observe her mother's daily ritual. Ever since I was a child, her mother's breath has smelled like stale booze.

"So," her mother says and places her hand on her hip. "How we doing on punch?"

The warm, sugary smell of zinfandel wafts from her tongue. Kelsey looks to her mother and impatiently shakes her head.

"Mom," she says. "You're slurring."

Her mother squints and stares at her daughter through black, beady eyes.

"Kkkelsey," she says and then pauses.

Kelsey taps her hand against her thigh and awaits the remainder of her mother's response. Instead, her mother lifts the lip of a translucent bowl and examines the sloshing virgin punch, apparently having forgotten what she meant to say.

"You girls have to drink more of this punch," she says and shuffles towards the liquor cabinet. She unscrews a bottle and pours herself a fresh drink.

Around the room, girls pair off and engage in mindless chitchat. Beside me, Kelsey sits on the floor and studies the blue carpeting.

"Did you really do that?" I say to her in a hushed tone.

"What? Talk back to my mom?" she says.

"No. Your stomach. Did you really do that?" I say.

Kelsey rubs her palm across the floor and looks up at me.

"You don't believe me?" she says.

"No, I do," I say, even though I'm not sure this is true. "I mean, I just feel like you would have told me something like that before. I just feel like I would have known."

"Well, I guess you don't know everything," she says. "If you don't believe me though, just ask my mom. I mean, she's right there."

She tilts her head toward her mother's turned back.

I part my lips to ask, and Kelsey looks at me with surprised, questioning eyes. Something in her stare stops me, and brings me to this simple fact: if Kelsey has spoken the truth, it means that, as a child, she attempted to take her own life. And if she has lied, it means that, for some reason, some part of her wants people to believe she wanted her life to end. I carefully weigh out my thoughts and become uncertain which is worse: a friend who wants to die, or a friend who wants people only to think she does. I stop myself before the words leave my mouth and reach for an acrylic party bowl instead. I place the salty chips onto my tongue. Some things, I conclude, are better left unsaid.

"No," I say. "I believe you."

Kelsey's mother clicks the cabinet doors shut, splashes her drink over the rim of her glass, and announces that the cake will be served soon.

"Fucking lush," Kelsey says under her breath and ladles herself a glass of the punch. She rolls her eyes as the sound of her mother's footsteps scuff away from the room.

Once her mother is gone, Kelsey sips her sherbet drink quickly, slams her cup onto the wooden coffee table and glides towards the liquor cabinet. She slides open the shuttered doors and a tube of fluorescent light springs to life. Slowly, she runs her hand across the paper labels on each bottle, selects one and untwists its cap.

"Time for more punch," she says, sarcastically. She shakes the bottle in front of her, like a toy, and pours a portion of the pale liquor into the bowl. The colors swirl together and become a muted shade of pink.

Kelsey passes plastic cups to each of her party guests. We smack our lips and squint at the mildly alcoholic taste. With every sip I take, the thought of Kelsey and pills and hospitals and purple cough syrup floats further into the peaks and valleys of my mind. We scream *hooray* for the birthday girl and decorate her body with pastel ribbons. We sit in a circle and anxiously listen to stories about tonguing and reaching second base. We press cold hands against warm, reddened cheeks. We dare one another to lift our shirts and run topless through the room.

By the time the bowl is near empty, our tongues and teeth stained neon, thoughts of sadness and lies and depression and death have been replaced with the gaiety of a strong buzz.

Together, in a teenage herd, we run towards the kitchen and giggle at nothing. Kelsey's white sheet cake is on the table; we ogle the fluffy frosting and chatter about the adorable pink and purple sugar florets. We stick gift-wrap bows to our heads, dance in place, and let the ribbons swing from side to side. We proudly announce to Kelsey's mother that we have polished off the punch, grin wildly and show off our ruby teeth stains. She stabs neon-colored candles into the cake, smiles, and takes a healthy sip from her glass. We sip, too, from our own glasses. Kelsey's sister, Erin, enters the kitchen and suspiciously eyes us. Her expression changes from happiness to frustration. A sigh of exhaustion escapes her and flutters her wispy brunette bangs. I wonder which frustrates her more: her mother's naivety or the fact that, as a teenager, Erin does not have control of the situation. She hugs Kelsey and poses with her for a quick photograph before she heads for the front door. Kelsey smashes her finger into the vanilla frosting and smears it across my face. She laughs. I laugh. Her mother laughs. The front door slams shut. We all laugh together in an inebriated haze.

Happy Birthday to You.

When only crumbs remain, and our glasses hold only a pale, pinkish residue, we crawl into our sleeping bags and chortle over stories of training bras and summer love. Our bellies full of sugar and our minds swirling in booze, we chuckle from beneath our quilts about this feeling — this blurred, out-of-body sense of nonchalance that, at ages thirteen and fourteen, we are all already so accustomed to.

Though some day, years from now, this moment will bring tears to my eyes. When I listen to new friends share childhood memories — stories of sleep away camps and cupcakes, their first sips of beer at age eighteen, I will think back on this moment with a dropping pain in the pit of me.

I will think about how different our childhood could have been.

But for now, I embrace this lightheaded feeling. I embrace my laughter as I think about Kelsey's story. *I had my stomach pumped once. Ha!* I embrace the hilarity of our flushed faces as we joke about braces and boys. But mostly, I embrace us — a group of girls, too young and too naive to realize that something within one of us might actually be very wrong.

Across the room, Katie releases a loud, throaty snore. Kelsey creeps from her sleeping bag, her hand pressed against her mouth to conceal her laughter, and playfully smacks a pillow across Katie's sleeping head. Katie's eyes jolt wide and, as she looks deliriously from side to side, Kelsey slips back beneath her sheets. The world seeming somewhat like a dream, we all giggle softly, our eyes heavy and fluttering. At some point while we are sleeping, Kelsey's mother sneaks downstairs and snaps a photograph. Despite the alcohol in our bellies or the questions about suicide that linger in our young minds, in the picture we will appear to be an innocent vision of a teenage slumber party. A perfect snapshot of an American cliché.

It is a Friday night sometime about mid-way through the eighth grade. Our friend, Amy, invites Kelsey and me to spend the evening at her home. At school, our classmates know Amy for her wild corkscrew curls and her willingness to kiss older boys. At home, Amy's Christian parents know their daughter as an innocent girl who believes in the power of God. What her parents do not know are the new methods Amy has found for getting in touch with her spirituality.

When Kelsey and I arrive, the three of us breeze through Amy's kitchen to collect armfuls of junk food. Along the way, Amy stops to kiss her mother and father gently upon their cheeks. She then pauses in front of an abstract painting that hangs on the wall. The painting was created by one of her parents' deceased friends. Her parents believe their friend still lives inside his painting, and, with his death, has become closer to God. Amy focuses on the painting, then lowers her eyes and begins to pray. Her parents watch this nightly routine with smiles of contentment.

Inside Amy's bedroom, we slip into cotton pajamas. Amy plugs in a set of dim white Christmas lights that dangle from the ceiling and presses a button on her stereo. Acoustic rock music hums softly through the room. Kelsey and I begin noisily to tear through bags of potato chips and Amy shushes us. She presses her ear against her bedroom door and patiently listens for the sound of her parent's footsteps. Once she hears their bedroom door click shut behind them, she jumps onto her bed.

"Thanks for coming over," she says. "The last time I did this, I was alone, and I started to freak out a little."

Amy reaches into a drawer and pulls out a sandwich bag filled with neatly rolled joints. She tosses them into my lap. Kelsey opens the window, sparks one of the joints and sucks in a deep drag. Amy crawls across the bed and joins us beside the window. In her hands is a small square of aluminum foil. She carefully unfolds it and then places a tiny paper tab onto her tongue. After a few seconds pass, she springs open her mouth to show us. When she does, the tab is gone.

"Now, we wait," Amy says and lights a joint of her own.

For the next hour, Kelsey and I pass joints and study Amy in anticipation. Though Kelsey and I have begun to find our own methods for clearing our heads, we rationalize that our new hobbies, unlike Amy's, are not entirely wrong. We believe that our drinking is just fine because, at any given time, we can march into Kelsey's home, rummage through her parent's cabinets, and take our pick from the collection of glistening bottles. We do not feel that pot is a problem, but more a teenage cliché. But, in Kelsey's eyes, and mine, Amy has taken things to a different level. This is a real drug. And although we are anxious to find new ways to spend weekend nights, we are not quite ready for this; it will be several years until we require anything with a similar effect.

For now, we huddle beside the icy window, smoking, and wait for Amy's hallucinations to begin. By the time the final joint has burned down to a stubby, black roach, Amy's eyes begin to shift crazily. Her back pressed firmly against her headboard, she speaks gibberish to no one in particular. In one instant, her eyes are closed and her head nodding, and in the next, her eyes are rolling toward the back of her head. In my hazy mind, I believe Amy has become possessed and for an instant, become afraid. I pour a capful of water into my palm and splash it on her. *The Body of Christ*, I say.

Her eyes wide, Amy fishes beneath her bed and pulls out a box of crayons. Without pausing to think about her actions, she begins to manically scribble a series of colorful, cartoon-like angels across her bedroom walls. In a stoned silence, Kelsey and I watch Amy as she colors in the angels' wings, and carefully runs her fingertips across their waxy features. Through a series of hardly coherent sentences, Amy tells us that one of the angel's wings has moved. Kelsey looks to me and laughs. When she does, my fear begins to disappear and my lips slowly part into a smile.

"They're only drawings," I say to Amy and point to the crayon she clutches in her hand. "They can't move. You created them yourself."

But Amy doesn't believe me and soon, the volume of her voice begins to increase. She grips chunks of her curls and tells us she fears the angels will fall from the walls and begin to flap frantically through her room.

"They're here for me," Amy says and tightly wraps a woven blanket around her head. "They're here for me because they know."

"Who's here for you?" Kelsey says. She lights a cigarette, coolly, turns to me and chokes back a laugh.

"The angels," Amy says. "It's like they can read my mind. Like they know what I've been thinking."

"Well, what have you been thinking?" I say, look to Kelsey and raise a judgmental brow.

"I've been thinking about death. I've been thinking about how sometimes, I'd really just like to die. I mean, what's the point of living, right, when I could die? When I could be closer to God, right? And the angels. They are the messengers and they heard me. And now they're here to take me away."

I glance at Kelsey and chuckle. Only this time, I notice I am laughing alone. Kelsey's face is focused exclusively on Amy's frightened expression.

"What do you mean you want to die?" Kelsey says, her tone dramatically different than it was just seconds ago.

"I don't know what I mean," Amy says. "Sometimes, I just hate myself. I hate everything about myself. I hate my face. I hate my body. I hate school. I hate my family. I don't see any purpose in it all."

Amy reaches her hand towards Kelsey.

"Do you ever feel like you want to die?" Amy says, slowly.

Kelsey exhales a thin stream of gray smoke.

"Sometimes," she says. "Sometimes, I hate myself, too."

And as she speaks these words, I cannot help but ask myself if she is kidding. If they are both kidding, and I simply do not get the joke. I, too, have spent hours critiquing my body and my personality. But death? I laugh, quietly, though neither Kelsey nor Amy avert their eyes from one another's faces. It is as though I am no longer here, sitting in the same room with them, at all.

"Sometimes, I just wish I could make it all go away," Kelsey says.

"You do?" Amy says and smiles. "Because sometimes, I just feel like I'm going crazy, you know? I don't want to feel sad, but sometimes, I just do."

A tear slides down Amy's cheek. She uncurls her fingers. A purple crayon rolls onto her bed.

"Do you ever think about the angels?" Amy says.

Kelsey takes a long pull from her cigarette and then balances the burning filter on the edge of the window frame. She settles down beside Amy on the bed.

"Sometimes I see angels," Kelsey says. "Sometimes I think about dying. I wonder about God and what comes after all of this. And sometimes, I wish I could make everything just go away for a while. Sometimes, I just wish I could die, too."

Later, when Amy's parents notice the angels, they will smile proudly, pleased to know their daughter's creative urges have spawned from something related to God.

As a teenager, all I wanted to do was hide. I wanted to hide from the hormones that raged through my body. From my friends and their developing hips and breasts. From the fact that my musical idol put a bullet through his brain. But mostly, I wanted the chance to hide, just for a moment, from myself.

Some weekends and holidays, my parents took me on brief excursions to other parts of our state. One particular New Year's Eve, my parents and I drove an hour and a half north to my aunt's home. My parents sparkled in their festive attire. My sister wore a glittery top and blew kisses as she dashed out the door to meet her friends. Before we left our home my mother pointed me to the few festive items in my closet.

"Ultimately, it's your decision," she said in her continual effort to support my creativity. "Just be yourself and wear whatever you'll feel most comfortable in," she said and gently closed my bedroom door behind her.

I slid each hanger across the metal closet rod, pausing to caress the various teenage identities that hung at the back of my closet behind my heavy winter coats. The preppy argyle cardigan. The trendy black shift dress with the shimmer overlay. The classic plaid mini-skirt and matching blue turtleneck. The delicate cashmere scarf. Sales tags dangled lifelessly from each of the unworn items. I slipped on the cardigan, remembering the day my father and I spent at the mall when I quietly asked him to purchase it for me. I allowed myself to admire my reflection, and the fact that with just one wardrobe swap I looked like the classic American girl I longed to be. I laughed at nothing and studied the giggling preppy girl who lived inside my mirror. She looked so charming, so wholesome, so carefree. She looked nothing like Kelsey. I pulled the cardigan from my body, rolled it into a ball and threw it to the floor.

I dug through my laundry pile and slipped on a faded t-shirt and

Kelsey's secondhand kilt, an outfit that was reminiscent of my friend and the false identity I tried so hard to establish for myself each day. I glanced at my reflection, satisfied that I could bring a piece of her with me for the evening, despite the fact that the whole ensemble made me feel out of place even before we arrived at the party.

As soon as I entered the foyer several of my female cousins, all about my age, threw their arms around me to express their excitement at my arrival. They wore glitter on their eyelids and pretty, age-appropriate dresses with sparkly tights, shimmering sweaters paired with sweet barrettes.

"Why aren't you wearing anything sparkly?" my cousin, Cristina, asked me, blowing on her freshly painted metallic fingertips while the others girls giggled at nothing.

"I mean, it's New Year's Eve," another cousin, Emma, said, adjusting her sequin headband and, without asking, grabbed hold of my hand. "We need to celebrate."

And with that, they escorted me upstairs, inviting me into their world of teenage normalcy. I reemerged as a new version of myself: one who wore her hair smoothed back in a glittering headband and defined her shape in a fitted festive blouse. I wanted to be mad at them for playing dress-up with me, but I never was. In the mirror that hung in my cousin's bedroom I saw the reflection of a young girl who had no need to hide — the reflection of the girl I wanted to be. When the ball dropped that evening, my cousins and I smoked candy cigarettes and watched the adults sip champagne. By the time the party ended, my desire to hide temporarily disappeared.

One Saturday, a few months shy of my fourteenth birthday, my mother and my aunt take Kelsey and me on a day trip across the bridge to Pennsylvania to spend the afternoon in a small artist's community. They allow us to wander the streets of the town on our own. For the next several hours, we browse in and out of shops and sip coffee from Styrofoam cups. We introduce ourselves to longhaired teenage boys on the street and join them for a smoke. We slip into a tattoo parlor and imagine what it would be like to one day have ink pressed into our skin.

In a small boutique, Kelsey and I play dress up, and drape our bodies in theatrical jackets, platform shoes and wigs. We adapt to the personas of our attire, and act like clichéd versions of disco dancers, British schoolgirls and pageant queens. We shimmy up and down the aisles of the store as if they are our own private runways, collecting boas and trendy caps along the way. When Kelsey's arms begin to overflow with silky shirts, she disappears behind a dressing room curtain. While I wait for her to burst back into the room wearing some colorful costume, I mindlessly browse through a variety of cluttered bins and stumble across a pair of vintage winged, rhinestone-encrusted sunglasses. Jokingly, I slip the non-prescription novelty glasses onto the bridge of my nose and allow my eyes to adjust to the feeling of seeing the world through frames. I blink dramatically and glance into a scratched mirror with the intention of laughing at my own image. But, when my reflection comes into view, I do not laugh. Rather, I am mildly pleased. The edges of my lips slowly lift into a smile.

For several moments I stare at the mirror, fascinated by the idea that, with just one simple accessory, I can begin to hide. These glasses, I decide, will act as a sort of shield for me. A ten-dollar plastic barrier to separate my face from other people's stares. Without speaking a word, I leave the glasses at rest on my nose, slip a bill onto the counter and wait for Kelsey outside beneath the shop awning.

From this day forward, I will wear these glasses almost daily, until finally, during high school, the plastic will crack and, for an instant, it will seem that I can see things clearly. I will throw the broken frames into a storage box that overflows with photographs, stuffed animals, and other childhood mementos. When I firmly snap the box's lid back into place, and thus say goodbye to my fractured frames, I will tell myself that there is nothing left to be fearful of. That there is nothing left from which I need to hide.

But years from then, when I learn that Kelsey is gone, one of the first things I will do, as though by instinct, is purchase a pair of similar thick-rimmed vintage frames. I will wear my new deep burgundy glasses religiously, convinced that, while they are on, the world cannot see who I really am. Through these glasses, I will tell myself, onlookers will be unable to see the churning emotions inside me. The loss I have endured. Behind these cheap frames, no one can see the thoughts that go on in my head. These glasses give me the courage to laugh at all the right moments and to give a firm handshake each time I meet someone new. They give me the strength to mingle with friends when all I really want to do is sob into my fists.

In my new disguise, I can maintain a certain distance between myself and the rest of the world. If I can hide my glassy, bloodshot eyes, I can convince everyone that I am okay. I can convince myself that I am okay. I can pretend to see life through new eyes: ones that do not know a world in which Kelsey existed.

With my glasses on, I will hide and learn to remerge as someone new. With my glasses on, I will raise my hand in class and share insights on Wordsworth and Blake and Burns and Keats, because my frames offer me a sense of protection. With my glasses on, I will believe that no one can observe the real me. The girl who is crumbling on the inside. The girl who locks herself in her dorm and stares for hours out a frosted pane of glass while creating "what if" situations in her head. The girl who will go on living her life as a question mark.

While working on an eighth grade school project in my family's garage, I accidentally cut my wrist. The shiny, silvery box cutter blade slices through my flesh, though I barely feel it. My delicate weapon is so seductive that it feels only like a tickle as it tears open my skin and gives way for crimson rivulets to flow down my hand.

Once I am stitched up and fine, my mother insists I stay home for several days to recuperate and to give the gossip that is centered on my ordeal a chance to blow over. She tells me people are going to make up stories about my unanticipated hospital trip, though doesn't provide the details of what she suspects they will say. I've already been through enough, she explains. It is better that I let things settle and allow the hallways time to begin to buzz with some other bit of teenage gossip before I return. However, I don't see what I need to recuperate from or why anyone would gossip about the few stitches in my wrist. The whole thing was an accident, like a scraped knee or a paper cut. But my mother is persistent. When I disagree, she blends frothy strawberry milkshakes to help sway me.

It is while I am home, indulging in mindless daytime TV, that my mother's point becomes clear to me. Our house phone begins to ring with surprising frequency. Teachers call to ask how I am coping. Mental health counselors and guidance counselors call to discuss my being at risk. Friends call and sob into the phone to confirm I am not dead. With the exception of Kelsey and my family, no one believes this was an accident. They've all pieced together certain facts — social outcast, razor blade, wrist — and created works of fiction to cling to.

But I don't want anyone to think I tried to take my own life. I want to stop these rumors before they run rampant through town. To cover the bloody gauze that peeks from my sweatshirt sleeve and explain to everyone that it wasn't my fault. To run through the school hallways and shout out that none of it was planned.

In my head I create scenarios in which I tell them all what really happened in a step-by-step account. I had been in my family's garage, surrounded by cardboard scraps and half-used cans of spray paint, contemplating ways to construct a design project for school (the same project many of my classmates had to design). I searched through the clutter, held out a triangular piece of cardboard, and pressed one end against my waist. The razor quietly slipped through the cardboard and, subsequently, my wrist, all in one quick motion. The blood rushed out of the u-shaped nick with each beat of my pulse. Already in shock, I calmly placed the cardboard and razor on a table, sought out my mother and told her that my wrist looked like a whale's spout, bursting with red water. Before I had a chance to fully comprehend the situation, I was spread across a waiting room sofa in the ER.

But now, I am in my living room, watching TV reruns, my body back to normal except for this throbbing in my wrist. And though I enjoy a few days away from school to indulge in bowls of macaroni and cheese, a part of me wishes that I were with my friends and teachers, explaining how scary the whole situation had really been. To describe the nurse who laid me down across a small cot and then asked me to stare at a mural of distorted cartoon characters while she slid the coarse thread through my skin. To tell them about the nurse who showed me just how close I was to cutting a major artery, and to describe the fear I experienced knowing I had been just inches from death. To explain how strange it feels to lose so much blood. How people speak, but nothing seems to make sense, and how when you look down at your injury your mind prevents you from registering that the damaged extremity is your own.

But, according to Kelsey, no one will believe me. She stops by my house each day after school to tell me so. From what she says, classrooms buzz with gossip about my failed suicide attempt.

"Jesus, you accidentally cut your wrist and you're a fucking celebrity," she says. "All anyone can talk about is how you tried to kill yourself."

"But that's not what I did. It was an accident," I say. "I slipped. You know that. Why would I want to be popular for that? Why would

I want people to think I tried to kill myself when all I did was have a slippery grip?"

"Was it *really* an accident?" Kelsey asks and raises a brow, seemingly intrigued by the idea that I might have the courage to commit to such a task.

"Of course it was!" I shout at her. "Why would anybody want to slice her own wrist?"

Kelsey pauses for a moment, perhaps contemplating my words.

"Well, whatever it was, you're definitely all anyone can talk about in school right now," she says, leans in close to me, and asks to see the place where I will scar.

I slowly lift the gauze, pulling strings of white fabric away from the black, zigzagged thread. Kelsey carefully observes the sewn up gash in my wrist. As she does this, I begin to think about *her* scars. The thin slashes of scab that crawl up her arms in neat, methodic designs.

Kelsey gently runs her fingers across the skin surrounding my solitary scab and chitchats about my recent surge in popularity. But as she speaks, all I can do is wonder if she feels envy towards me at this moment; if she is jealous of the attention my singular scar has received.

I wonder if Kelsey wishes that she too could have an accident. If she wishes her phone would ring for days from people who pray she is still alive. But mostly, I wonder if she wishes she had the courage to cuff up her shirtsleeves and show them the series of scarlet cuts patterned all across her milky skin. If she wishes she had the courage to expose the details of her nightly affair with a worn razor blade to someone other than me.

A fan of pastel paint chips is spread across my new bedroom carpet. Stacked along the walls are the few remaining cardboard moving boxes and rolled up posters I brought with me from my previous bedroom. It has only been a few weeks since our family has moved into our new home, though we all agree that we are happy in this space. A decorative chandelier hangs in our foyer. A crystal vase of fresh cut flowers is set in the center of our new kitchen island. A white wooden porch swing gently rocks outside our front door. Despite the fact that it is nearly summer, warm flames flicker each evening in our new fireplace.

The biggest change, however, that will result from our recent move has nothing to do with home furnishings. Although it was not a specific factor in their real estate search, the home my parents selected ultimately decided my high school fate. In a few months, after we graduate the eighth grade, Kelsey and I will be forced to attend different schools for the first time in our lives. She will spend the next four years at a school that is commonly listed at the bottom of school rating lists. Even though we only moved a few miles, I will now be fortunate enough to attend one of the best pubic high schools in our state. It is the place that will influence my college choices; the place where I will meet many of my lifelong friends; the place where I will first meet the man I will later marry.

My mother and I sit beside one another and sort through the paint colors while sipping herbal tea. We joke as we point out hideous shades of pinks and greens and then finally agree upon a yellow-striped strip. We extend the strip before us and begin to squint and tilt our heads while we imagine a feminine butter-hued room.

"What do you think?" my mother asks as she presses the paint chip against a bare white wall.

"I like it," I say but then quickly hesitate. "Well, I don't know. Is it too girly? Won't it look stupid behind all my posters?" I ask and nod to the pile of rock posters and bohemian tapestries that sit in a neat pile.

"I don't think so," she says, reaches for a lavender paint chip and compares the two colors. "Who knows if you'll want to put all those things back on the walls, anyway. You may be happy with just a fresh coat of paint."

I offer her a judgmental glare.

"Look," she says. "You're the one who has to live in here so you need to be the one who is happy with the final product. It's entirely your choice. We don't even have to paint if you don't want to."

I glance back at the pile of miscellaneous wall art I've accumulated over the past few years.

"No," I tell her. "I like the yellow. It's pretty. It looks cheerful."

She smiles in agreement and then begins to move through the room, clearly envisioning the final product as she holds the strip against a honey-colored dresser, a wooden chest and a blue quilt that rests on my bed.

"It's going to look nice," she says. "I think you'll really like it."

She places the paint chip on my nightstand and brushes a strand of hair away from my face.

"It will be a good color for you to grow into," she says.

That evening Kelsey and I sit across from my parents at my family's kitchen table. My mother ladles spoonfuls of homemade macaroni and cheese onto each of our plates, pours glasses of pink lemonade and passes a glass bowl filled with steaming biscuits. My sister, who works at a local office and still lives at home with our family, lingers in a corner of the kitchen and finishes a phone call with a friend.

"What are you girls up to this weekend?" my father asks Kelsey and me while motioning to my sister to finish her call.

Kelsey scoops a heaping forkful of macaroni into her mouth.

"Me and my dad are painting my bedroom," she explains.

"Hey, that's pretty cool," he says. "Did you girls plan to both makeover your rooms at the same time?

"Sort of," Kelsey says. "At least, I think my dad and I are going to do it this weekend or next. You can never really be sure with him."

"We just thought it'd be kind of fun," I say. "You know, for both of us to change things up a bit."

"Well, it sounds like a good time," my dad says.

"Yeah, it should be pretty cool. You know, assuming the old man can hold the brush steady," Kelsey says, which sends the two of us into a fit of laughter.

The phone rings. My sister uses the awkward pause in conversation as an opportunity to answer the call. In the background, she whispers her evening plans to a friend. Both my parents are quiet, unconcerned that my sister has left the table, their attention centered exclusively on Kelsey. We are all accustomed to Kelsey's constant jokes about her parents and their alcoholism and her habit of using sarcasm as a defense. However, I am still too ignorant to comprehend the obvious concern that should be connected with these habits. Instead, I simply note the facts. Based on my observations Kelsey's parents are *indeed* alcoholics who seem to dismiss many of their daughter's brief phrases, small gestures and seemingly miniscule behaviors. The same phrases and gestures and behaviors that, due to my own adolescent naivety, I also tend to dismiss. Only later would I learn that they were the same short-lived moments my own parents often spent days analyzing.

Kelsey casually helps herself to a second serving as my parents wait in anticipation for her to add any further details to her story. They are cautious never to verbalize their judgments about Kelsey's family. Nor do they criticize her actions or her appearance or the fact that she laughs every time she shares stories about her home life. Instead, they listen to every word she is willing to share and compile mental inventories of her stories in preparation, perhaps, for the day Kelsey finally stops laughing and admits the truth of her pain.

"So what color did you pick?" my mother asks in an effort to make the conversation more positive.

Kelsey rips apart a biscuit and uses it to sop up the cheesy sauce that puddles her plate.

"Black," she says.

"Black?" my mother immediately questions. "Kelsey, you don't want to do that."

"Why?" Kelsey asks.

"Because it will close off the whole room. A color that dark will make it feel claustrophobic in there."

"What do your parents think?" my father asks. "Everything else aside, I can't imagine they'd be excited to have to paint over black walls."

"Well," Kelsey says through a smirk. "I sort of had a certain strategy when convincing them."

"And what was that strategy exactly?" my father asks.

Kelsey and I exchange glances and resume our laughter.

"I just asked them about it when they were both drunk," Kelsey says. "They probably don't even remember what color we agreed on."

"Kelsey," my mother says. She sighs as she searches for the right words and then becomes quiet when she realizes there are none.

"You have to admit," I say. "It was pretty clever."

My parents stare at one another from across the table while Kelsey and I continue to convulse with amusement. My sister slides back into her seat. As our laughter dies down, Kelsey reaches for her fork. My mother places her hand on top of Kelsey's and squeezes it for just a second. Unsure of how to remedy Kelsey's situation, my father excuses himself from the table and reappears with five bowls of ice cream.

Outside the kitchen windows the sky fades from daylight to dusk. My mother begins to clear the table. My father licks his spoon, moves closer to Kelsey and playfully tousles her hair.

"Come on, kiddo," he says. "How about I give you a lift home before it gets too late? We can throw your bike in the trunk of my car."

Kelsey nods and begins to move towards the sink.

"Dinner was awesome, as always," she says. "Thanks for having me."

"You know you don't have to thank us for stuff like that, Kel," my mother says. "You know you're always welcome here."

"I know," Kelsey says. "But thanks, anyway."

"Have fun painting your room," my mother says.

Kelsey turns to walk away but then quickly pivots back.

"Do you really think black is going to look weird?" she asks.

"Well, it wouldn't be my first choice," my mother says honestly. "It just seems kind of depressing, that's all. I just want to see you create a space for yourself that will make you feel happy."

"I think it will make me feel happy," Kelsey reassures her.

My mother gently caresses a piece of hair that dangles in front of Kelsey's face.

"I'm certain whatever color you pick will look beautiful," she says.

Kelsey smiles, squeezes herself against my mother's body and briefly closes her eyes.

"I love you," Kelsey says.

"I love you, too, Kel," my mother says. "Get a good night's sleep. I'll see you soon."

Kelsey and her father begin to renovate her bedroom on a Saturday. I spend the morning at school, dressed in costume and caked makeup, to rehearse my part in the end-of-the-year school production of *Give My Regards to Broadway,* an extracurricular activity Kelsey chose not to be a part of, despite her creative talents. On my walk to Kelsey's house, I practice my character's thick, New York accent. In my mind, this accent makes me sound tougher than I really am.

When I enter Kelsey's room, it immediately summons childhood images of a haunted mansion. Outlines of furniture exist beneath draped, cream-colored sheets. Walls are haphazardly coated with a dark, saturated shade. An entire wall is covered with holes and thin, web-like cracks that spread from them like traces of thread. From a small window, a beam of sunlight stretches across the floor. I study the tube of light, afloat with particles of dust. This single ray is all that remains of the room that existed amongst these walls only yesterday.

Kelsey and her father are hard at work, popping open cans and slapping new layers of paint on the already darkened walls. Her father slams a sledgehammer through the wall, rests the tool at his side, and crumbles a piece of drywall in his hand. He glances at my gaping expression.

"Does it look that good?" he asks and smiles.

He pulls a pack of cigarettes from the pocket of his frayed denim shorts and adjusts his mesh cap.

"Your friend here picked out the color. Looks pretty cool, doesn't it?" he says.

When he exhales, a grayish cloud of smoke is sucked into the demolished wall behind him.

Aside from the battered wall, the room is almost completely covered in a shade of deep eggplant. The muddy color is spattered across Kelsey's skin and clothing; it drips from her in thick, fat drops.

Kelsey's father lifts his hat, wipes his hairline and reaches for his acrylic tumbler. I call this his Saturday tumbler, as, on weekends, the cocktail-filled cup never leaves his hand. He sips from it, smacks his lips and smiles with satisfaction.

"So this here," he says and bangs his fist against the wall. Puffs of whitish dust float from the cracks. "This will be our shadow box," he says. "Like a secret hole in the wall where you two can hide anything you like."

He crouches, lifts a screwdriver, and pries the gleaming metal top from a gallon of paint. He dips and twirls his finger in the can.

"When it's done, we'll paint it with this," he says and lifts his black-coated finger. The color trickles to the floor like drops of motor oil.

I wonder now about what didn't dawn on Kelsey's parents back then: the fact that, when complete, the entire room would resemble the beginning stages of a deep, painful bruise.

Kelsey, her father and I work all afternoon, busying ourselves with sandpaper and rollers, dedicated to covering any traces of innocence that peek through the drying paint. Kelsey's mother carries in a bowl of potato chips and a pitcher of sweetened iced tea. Kelsey's father tunes the radio to a classic rock station, sparks a cigarette and pats his daughter on the head. Erin periodically stops in to see our progress. Each time she does her face contorts to an expression of shock as she witnesses the dark color slowly consuming the room. We all tease her for being too uptight, laugh and smear paint across each other's cheeks. Just outside the window, car tires spin past, children scream, soccer balls echo as they are shot into garbage can goals. Out there, the world seems as it should. In here, the early stages of a disease spread themselves across the walls.

Outside, the sky has faded to navy. Streetlamps cast an orange glow across the road on the opposite side of the window frame. The streets have begun to fall quiet. Our brushes have been laid down. I lie across the floor, listening as the stereo quietly hums with the music of a local garage band.

Kelsey glides across the room and runs her fingers over dried patches of the walls.

"Can you believe they let me do this?" she whispers.

She switches on a desk lamp with no shade; its glow casts distorted shadows across the walls and ceiling. Kelsey lies down beside me, stretches, and inhales deeply to savor the dizzying smell of fresh paint. The stereo deck clicks off. We sit in silence for several seconds, listen to the quiet pulling sounds of the tape, and wait for the flip side to begin.

"I could spend my whole life in this room," she says and smiles at her creation.

The sounds of an acoustic guitar echo softly. I close my eyes and let the notes drift though my head.

"I could sit all day and all night inside this purple room," Kelsey says.

Years later, she would.

It is the last week of summer, a wicked August afternoon that makes your skin drip just from standing still. Kelsey and I spend the morning as we do most summer mornings. We walk mindlessly through town and, with fat black pens, mark our names on the walls of buildings. We sneak through the back lots of shopping centers, take turns pushing one another in wobbly carts, and ultimately crash into curbs. We stop into an old-fashioned ice cream shop and drink strawberry malts until we think our brains might freeze. By lunchtime, our t-shirts are wet with perspiration, and spots of sunshine blacken our vision. We decide to stop off at the closest place we can find to briefly find refuge from the heat.

The aisles of the beauty supply shop overflow with candy-colored beauty products packaged in plastic and in glass. Rainbows of petite polish bottles line pre-made display racks, rows of color that spread from indigo to burgundy to brown. Kelsey and I brush our fingertips over the labels of Mane & Tail shampoo, gallons of mango and cocoa body lotion and jars of lemon cuticle crème. We glide across the floor, as though possessed by the acetone smell that seeps from every crevice of the shop.

Kelsey pulls off her knit beret and shakes her head. Several thin, red braids fall and frame her face. She strokes one of them between her fingers and lets out a short puff of a sigh.

"I'm ready for a change," she says and rolls her eyes to examine the strawberry blonde strands.

We peruse the shelves slowly, icy air blowing across our damp necks. We take our time to shake and sample bottles of glittery polish, dabbing beads of sweat from our faces before we swipe the color across our toenails. A twenty-something salesgirl sits at the front counter and eyes us from behind the cover of a glossy magazine. She snaps her gum loudly and twirls a piece of her over-processed hair around her fingertip.

"You girls looking for something?" she says and breathes heavily, exhausted by her efforts.

Kelsey squeezes a glob of ice blue serum into her palm and runs it through the hair at the nape of her neck. I pose momentarily beside a yellowed mannequin, her fake, plastic head trapped beneath a giant bubble-shaped dryer.

"Nope," Kelsey says. "We've got everything covered over here."

She mists coconut body spray into the air and dances beneath the fragrant cloud, as though it is rain.

I follow Kelsey as she breezes towards a back aisle, waving my hands in front of me to help the fresh polish dry. As I do this, I study Kelsey's movements: The way her bag slaps her side each time she takes a step. The way she pouts her lips and tilts her head with wonder while she browses through acrylic nail kits. The way she rests her hand on her hip and pulls a braid across her lips. But mostly, I think about how alone I will feel without her. Next week, high school will begin and, for the first time in our lives, we will be separated. Town lines have marked our fate. She will move to the left and I will move to the right. We will sharpen our pencils each day on opposite ends of town.

For the next four years Kelsey will drift through hallways filled with many of the same faces from our grammar school. The same girls who will settle in our town before their lives even start. As I silently watch Kelsey, I wonder what the next four years will be like for me. Out of the roughly 1,000 students who attend my new high school, I know less than a half dozen of them. I think about my mother's many pep talks. *A fresh start. A chance to reinvent yourself.* The truth is that is exactly what I'd like to do. I'm ready to become someone that people notice. I want boys to think I am pretty and ask me to school dances. I want teachers to smile as they describe the success they are certain I will find. I want to meet friends who I can daydream with about college applications and summer travel. Friends who will share my excitement to organize study groups and volunteer groups and …

I want these things for Kelsey, too. I crave a sense of normalcy for us both.

Kelsey pauses beside a shelf lined with countertop mirrors,

various sized ovals situated across it like a funhouse wall. As she moves forward, her face spreads from mirror to mirror. She narrows her eyes, observes her many reflections and combs her fingers through her hair. My stomach aches as I wonder what it will be like to wander the halls of some new building without her. I swipe my greasy palms down the fronts of my denim cutoffs, leaving behind a faint lotion stain. As I step closer to Kelsey, she moves away, preoccupied by a display of tortoise shell combs. Now, *my* reflection multiplies across the shelf. I pause, smile a half smile at myself and slide a tube of ruby red lipstick across my lips.

"Down here," Kelsey whispers from the end of the aisle.

Amid paddle brushes and economy-sized cans of aerosol hair spray is row upon row of synthetic hair — coarse, one-inch strips, organized according to color, from silver to platinum to auburn to brown. Kelsey and I rub the samples between the pads of our fingertips, squat down and press them against our foreheads. We imagine how much more interesting life would be for us as blondes.

Kelsey crouches and begins to fumble through tubs stacked on the bottom shelves. Unlike the other coloring kits, these tubs do not have colorfully displayed pieces of rough hair, but rather, are concealed in generic, white containers, like some dirty secret the storeowners are ashamed to admit. She unscrews the cap and reveals a thick paste the color of a Caribbean sea. Her eyes widen and she laughs a malicious belly laugh, the sort reserved for occasions like this, when she knows she is about to be up to no good. I lean down beside her and stick my finger into the dye.

"This," Kelsey says, "is just the kind of change I'm looking for."

We swipe the dye across our palms and envision our faces beside wild hair colored in magenta, fuchsia, or lime. One by one, we uncap new jugs, bright hues of electric purple and blue and green that surround us like a piece of pop art. Kelsey's eyes glitter with anticipation.

"Help me pick out one you like," she says.

"My mother will murder me if I dye my hair with any of these," I say.

Kelsey skims her finger across the backside of one of the tubs.

92

"No she won't. Not if I do it with you," Kelsey says.

She remains quiet as she waves the open jar beneath my chin.

"So," she says. "You in?"

I nod. Sure, I think. I'm in.

Kelsey spins one of her braids like a tiny lasso.

"It's about time to say goodbye to strawberry blonde," she says.

We drop two plastic tubs of hot pink dye onto the counter and wait while the saleswoman finishes reading about orgasms and pant hems. She lays the open magazine down with a sigh, examines our purchases and places them into a plastic bag.

"You girls know you need brushes for these, right?" she says and pops her wad of bubblegum with a loud snap.

Kelsey and I shrug and toss our crumpled singles and coins onto the counter.

"They're in the back," the woman says and sighs again. She leans across the counter and points towards the far end of the shop. "They look just like mini paint brushes."

She looks down at the cover of her magazine, anxious to return to her reading.

"Look. Just go grab one and I'll pretend I didn't see anything," she says and shuts her register drawer. She picks up the magazine and flips to a new page, returning to the glossy world of her dreams.

Kelsey's parents are at work for the afternoon so we set up shop in their laundry room, converting the sink into a rinsing station, the dryer lid into a miniature beauty display. I lean my head into the sink and allow Kelsey to splash my hair, warm water trickling down my jaw line and across my cheeks. My heart races as I think about my mother, and the furious reaction I am certain she will have. But more so, I think about the camaraderie this moment brings for Kelsey and me. That each time I receive a judgmental stare from a new classmate, I will know that someone, somewhere, is experiencing the same thing.

"My mom's going to murder me," I say again.

But Kelsey pretends not to hear me over the rushing sound of water. Instead, she looks at me with a smirk and massages her fingers into my scalp. When my whole head is damp, she tugs the hair at the nape of my neck and lifts my dripping head from the sink.

Kelsey scoots herself onto the washing machine and sips warm beer from a can. I stand beside her, waiting like a child on Christmas morning, anxious for her to unscrew the tub and reveal our selection. She uncaps it slowly, full of suspense, and exposes the goopy, pinkish shade. *Radiant-Red Violet*.

I sit on a folding chair in the center of the room, the floor and my shoulders lined with bath towels. Kelsey begins to paint small sections of my hair neon pink, while the room fills with a stinging ammonia scent. Once my hair is saturated with chemical color, we switch places. Now, Kelsey sits in the middle of the room and taps her foot in anticipation.

"You know," I say. "It's something like only two percent of people have natural red hair like yours."

"So what's your point?" she says and lights a cigarette.

"Are you sure you want to say goodbye to it for good?" I say.

"It'll grow back," she says.

"Yeah, but, it will never be exactly the same. It's like when you lose your virginity. You can go a while without having sex, but you'll never be a virgin again," I say, as though I have any experience with the topic.

"Trust me. I'm ready," she says. "I want to be a new version of myself. I don't want to look like me anymore."

She tosses her lit cigarette into the damp sink.

"I don't care what the statistics say," she says. "I'm ready to become someone new."

I dip the brush into the dye and smear a thick line of pink down her center part.

"Goodbye strawberry blonde," I whisper to her head and spread the color across her crown.

When the egg timer buzzes, we both rush to the sink and furiously rub our fingers through our hair, a puddle of red-tinted water swirling near the drain. Kelsey presses a towel against her head. Her curls fall delicately and frame her face. Even through the dampness, I can see that her natural hair color has been transformed to a rich shade of sultry pink, a candy-colored version of Hollywood red. Instantly, she embraces her new character and seductively shakes her hair the way women do in movies, just before they make love.

"You look like a star," I say and slip my fingers through her wet strands.

The front door clicks shut. Erin walks downstairs to greet us.

"Holy shit," she says.

"Does it look that good?" Kelsey says.

"Your mom is going to kill you," Erin says and looks at me.

"Is it that noticeable?" I ask nervously.

"Your head is pink," she informs me.

"Well, what about your mom?" I say.

The two sisters stare at each other in silence for a moment and then burst into laughter at some private joke.

"Come on," Erin says and playfully grabs my shoulder. "You've been in our house long enough to know that neither of our parents are going to say a damn thing."

Outside, Kelsey and I sit like starlets. We dangle our feet over the edge of the pool. Ice shaped as half-moons jangles in our cocktail tumblers. Black, oval sunglasses cover our eyes. I swirl my feet through the water, sip my drink, and turn toward Kelsey. When I do, I catch a glimpse of my reflection in her lenses.

I know the moment I walk through my door, my mother will scream and my father will look at me with an expression of disappointment. I know that in just a few days, I will move through the halls of some strange, new building, void of familiar faces, and receive many unwelcome stares. But right now, during this singular moment, as I shift my eyes between my reflection and Kelsey's head to observe the similarity in our appearances, I pretend that we are one. Our strengths and our weaknesses combine to create one perfect person. And with this thought, nothing else seems to matter.

I reach out my arm and touch one of Kelsey's curls.

"We've never looked the same before," I say and withdraw my hand.

Kelsey lights two cigarettes and places one between my lips. She fingers a strand of my hair. For what feels like hours, we blow thin streams of smoke toward each other's faces. And here, beneath the humid August sunlight, we study the striking new resemblance that we share.

How do you describe a disease you cannot see? A disease you cannot touch. Cannot feel the rotting flesh, or the patchy, balding scalp. How do you describe this thing that does not seem real:

This invisible sickness.

Do you describe the scaly, self-inflicted scabs you convince yourself are the result of an accidental fall? The violent mood swings you tell yourself are from hormones. The hours spent hidden beneath bed sheets, hiding from nothing. From everything. The hours you tell yourself are the result of a common flu.

How do you close the storybook you've created in your mind and finally admit that the one thing in life that scares you most — the thing you've convinced yourself is embedded in a world of pretend — is real, and is becoming more so with each passing day?

As an adult, people ask me, "How did Kelsey die?" I have my formulated answer that I provide them: she was depressed. But it was so much more than that. The violent mood shifts that were the result of her bi-polar disease and her even more violent schizophrenic personality shifts. The voices she claimed to hear and the fictitious people she claimed to know. The sadness. The anger. The confusion. The physical pain she caused herself each time she cut her skin or used a drug or a drink as a band-aid.

Once Kelsey was gone, I decided the best thing for me would be to start a new life. To simply return to college and cut all ties with her family and all of our mutual friends. To hide photographs and cassette tapes and anything that might make me think of my life with her. But many nights, as I sat staring out my dorm room window at the icy campus green, I would wonder about her death. I knew only some of the facts: she was sad, she swallowed too many pills and then she was gone. But were her actions intentional? A joke gone awry? An accident? Or did she really crave her own death so much that she was willing to put the rest of us through so much pain?

The autopsy results were scheduled to arrive the same day I was scheduled to move back into my dorm. By then, I had already severed all my ties. I never called her family to ask about the outcome.

High school. Busy with my new schedule, my new school and my new friends, I haven't seen or spoken to Kelsey in weeks. My phone rings and wakes me from a deep sleep. I groggily fumble for the receiver and am surprised to hear her on the other end. Her breath is consumed by violent sobs. Before I even say hello, she begins to ramble about a boy named Sam. Kelsey claims she met Sam, who is several years her senior, while vacationing in a small beach town over a year ago. They spent a few nights together on the beach and kissed beside the crashing waves. Kelsey and Sam have not seen each other in months, though in recent weeks, she claims she has begun to call him with increasing regularity.

"He says it's over," Kelsey says and tries to catch her breath. "He says we're through."

"Wait, what do you mean?" I say, still fuzzy with sleep. "What's through?"

"Us," she says. "Sam and I. He says we're done."

"Oh. Well, what *were* you exactly?" I say.

But Kelsey says nothing. Rather, she sobs violently into the phone.

"I thought he loved me," she says, her voice broken as she gulps for air. "I thought he was the one."

I have never heard Kelsey cry like this before. In truth, I have never heard her express any sort of emotion like this before. It is as though years of pent up feelings, anger, frustration and pain have exploded inside her and now spill down her face in the form of tears. I wonder if this conversation is really about Sam, or if there is something more.

I look at my clock. Green digital numbers pulse with the time. It is the middle of the night, just a few hours short of dawn.

"It doesn't matter though," Kelsey says, her voice still fighting to overcome her tears, "because he told me tonight that he's getting married and that I have to leave him alone."

I try to reassure Kelsey, remind her how beautiful she is, and how one day she will meet a man who is better than Sam ever was. I tell her Sam is a fool, even though I've never met him, and therefore am not sure that he is. In truth, I am not even certain if he exists.

"You'll meet someone else," I say.

But this is not what Kelsey wants to hear. The piercing sound of her scream vibrates through the phone.

"Why don't you understand?" she shouts. "Why can't you fucking understand? There's never anyone else. I'm the only one who'll never find someone else. Not you. Not our friends. I'm the only one who doesn't have what you all have."

I try to interrupt her, but she continues to scream through the line.

"You'll never understand *this*. You'll never understand what I feel. What I'm trying to say. I'm the only one who is going to end up alone."

And before I have the chance to ask her what she means, she slams down the phone.

The next day, I receive a call from Kelsey's mother. Her voice quivers as she speaks.

"You're going to need to come over," is all that she says on the phone.

When I arrive at the house, I will learn the beginning details of Kelsey's first hospital stay.

"I'd like to try a form of hypnosis on you," the doctor says. "I'd like to try and help you to remember."

*Remember.* The word flutters through me, and makes each individual cell in my body seem to pulse. The flesh of my wrists. The softness of my neck. The heaviness of my chest. My pulse increases and every part of my body begins to pound.

But here is what I would like to remember: how did I ever even allow myself to forget? When did I give permission to my brain to hide my memories of her? To dismiss any stored images of her face and her body? To begin to completely wipe the thought of her away?

I have become fascinated in recent months by the mysteriousness of the body. How mine works to protect me, unwillingly forcing my memory loss upon me as a final form of self-defense. *Don't think of those things*, my mind seems to scream at me. *You're too fragile. They are too much for you to handle.* And so, apparently knowing better than I do, my body has exorcised me of nearly every moment I shared with her.

The doctor fingers a small bronzed bell and instructs me to close my eyes and just *listen.* I want to explain to the doctor that, for months now, I have tried to listen. I have listened to old albums that, at one time, reminded me of her. I have listened to the advice of family and friends, and calmly closed my eyes to try and visualize her face. I have listened to myself sob late in the evenings, my cheeks wet, as I have tried to recall some piece of her without the assistance of a photograph.

But my brain fights me. It keeps many of my memories neatly stored in some place I cannot find. And the gentle tap of a miniature bell will not do the trick. I need to have a giant gong rung in my ears to help stimulate my uncooperative mind.

"Just close your eyes," the doctor says. "And listen to the sound of your breath."

I lower my lids and attempt to concentrate on the expansion of my lungs. *In. Out. In.*

*Ting.* The bell rings softly, though my mind is not clear. A million insignificant thoughts stream through my head. *Is there enough change in the parking meter? Did I turn off the stove?*

Yet, as I've predicted, not one of these thoughts relates to her.

My heart begins to flutter with anxiety. I try to stay focused on my breathing, embarrassed that the doctor will sense my panic attack and thus my weakness.

"Tell me what you see," the doctor says.

I assume that the doctor expects me to be flooded with once distant memories of my friend. To begin to describe long forgotten moments that will translate to have a deeper, more profound meaning. But my mind is veiled in black. There is only a blank screen where Technicolor images of the two of us once lived.

"Nothing," I say and quietly accept my failure.

For a moment, I imagine my body shattering, like glass, and crashing onto the floor. But no liquid rushes from inside my fragile shell. I am empty. There is nothing left in me at all.

*Ting.* The bell rings and its vibrations quietly carry through the room. I think about the sound it makes, how similar it is to the voice of a child, so soft and yet so piercing. *Does it sound like her voice,* I wonder. But I don't recall details like this anymore. I try to refocus my thoughts, though my mind is consumed by the gentleness of the ring. I imagine that, if I could see sound, it would appear like smoke. Soft, muted spirals of gray that float before me until they begin to fade and vanish.

"Breathe," the doctor says and I concentrate on the hollow noise of my breath. I think about my body and how it expands and contracts. I begin to wonder if this doctor can help mend me. If she holds the power to take all these broken pieces and make me feel whole again.

But mostly, I think of *her* body, just before it collapsed. Did she feel her final breath leave her? Did she feel herself beginning to slip away? And just as I start to think of these things, I see it.

"I see color," I say. "I can see bursts of red."

As these words slip from my lips, the bursts begin to congeal and mold themselves into one coherent shape.

"It's her car," I say. "I can see Kelsey's car."

The memory comes trickling back to me. The day Kelsey's parents proudly parked their daughter's new red convertible in their drive. The happiness that spread across Kelsey's face as she imagined the strong sense of independence having her own vehicle would provide.

"Why do I see her car and not her?" I say in a panic.

But the doctor remains calm.

"Just keep breathing," she says. "Take whatever your mind gives you."

With a few more breaths, my head begins to explode with color. Splashes of purple and green and gold blend with the red, like splatters across a canvas.

"We are driving," I say. "Just Kelsey and I."

In my mind the vision begins to become clear. The top of Kelsey's convertible is pressed down. Sunlight pours across both our shoulders. Our hair flaps wildly in the breeze. And then, I hear her voice:

"Do you love it?" Kelsey says.

I reach out my hand and touch her arm.

"I absolutely love it," I say and then pat my palm against the dash. "She's a red head, just like you."

The car accelerates and, as it does, I am able to make out the landscape that surrounds us. A clear blue sky. A stretch of flat road ahead. Kelsey turns to me and smiles. She shifts her black sunglasses from the crown of her head and covers her eyes.

"I'm really happy," she says, and I know that she means it.

Kelsey and I discuss the many adventures we will seize in her new car. Saturday afternoon trips to the shore. Weekend adventures into the city. Midnight drives in autumn to hear the sound of rustling husks.

And in my mind, Kelsey and I believe these things. We believe that this new car will change everything. That with it, Kelsey will be able to drive away from her illness, away from the doctor's visits, away from the hospital stays, away from all the pills. That I will be able to drive far away from our town and into a life framed by normalcy. As the two of us travel alone, on this long expanse of pavement, the air blowing across our skin, the weight of recent times has managed to melt away. Street signs rush past. The radio hums. In this moment, these are the only things that matter. Out here, on this open road, there is no sickness. There is no pain. There are no questions. There is only us and the road ahead and the prospect of driving away from it all.

# The End

Some days, after the 2:30 high school bell rings and the hallways empty, I walk home alone, watch TV, and then pretend something terrible is wrong with me.

From time to time, I pretend to be pregnant at age 15. I stuff pillows and rolled up sweaters beneath my t-shirts and model the look in a hallway mirror. I run my hand over my fictitious belly, force out dramatic sobs, and explain to my reflection how difficult it will be to raise a bastard child in such a cruel, miserable world.

Now and again, upon finishing my afternoon snack, I retreat to the bathroom and comb electric blue gel through my hair. My locks shine with grease. In my bedroom, I pretend to be a teen runaway, and tell my audience of teddy bears and porcelain dolls about the woes of life on the street.

On some days, I light candles, spread them across my dressers, and pull down my bedroom window shades. I insert an album into my stereo. The speakers hum with acoustic strums and mournful lyrics. My eyes shut, I lip-sync into a round hairbrush and try to imagine pain so deep I am compelled to share it with a crowd.

But on most afternoons, before my family arrives home, I sift through the contents of my mother's makeup bag, lift myself onto her bathroom countertop and sweep thick circles of eggplant, navy, and plum shadows around my eyes. I smudge ebony powder onto my cheekbones, and wipe thick streaks of it across my neck. I press the spongy applicator into the inner corners of my eyes and watch as charcoal-colored dust floats through forming tears. I blink and the tears are released. For minutes, I stare blankly at my reflection, comforted by the image of make-believe black and blue marks on my skin.

As a teenager, I yearn for something to be wrong with me. For a mother who puts me down. For a boyfriend who forces himself upon me and then whispers, "Baby, it'll be okay." For a father who raises his hand to me, rather than what I do have — a father who makes my childhood teddy bear stylishly dance across my belly to help lift me from a sour mood.

So many nights, Kelsey calls me to report all the things in her life she deems wrong. Her grades. An argument with her father. Her inability to find beauty in her own face.

"I fucking hate my life," she says.

Her anger sounds so authentic. Knowing that Kelsey experiences a constant sense of sadness in her day-to-day life, and that I do not, brings me a constant sense of guilt. Now that Erin, Kelsey's only ally in her home, has moved more than an hour away for college, Kelsey is more alone than ever before. I want to understand how she feels so I can comfort her and bring a deeper sense of camaraderie to our relationship. I want to offer her any source of comfort that I can.

I press the phone to my ear and reflect on my choreographed moments of fake sadness and then agree with Kelsey, telling her how messed up life is, how nobody understands, how we should run away together to some new town far away from here.

"I fucking hate my life, too," I say.

But Kelsey sees right through me.

"Don't give me that shit," she says. "You don't fucking hate your life at all. I bet right now you're in your living room eating a bowl of ice cream while your parents watch TV."

I lick my spoon and guiltily place down my bowl.

"I'm sorry," I say. "I was just trying to — "

"Don't be sorry," she says. "I wish I had what you have."

But the truth is, I am sorry. I am sorry that I have a boyfriend and Kelsey does not. I am sorry each time my parents offer me an extra afghan to keep warm. I am sorry at the end of each school term when my progress reports bear only words of praise. I am sorry that Kelsey has no sense of an ally in her home now that her sister has started college in a different part of the state. And so, on some afternoons, when no one else can see, I wipe dusty streaks of pewter and scarlet across my eyelids, cheeks, and throat. I am desperate to experience pain. I yearn to feel something real, though it will be years until I finally do. And so, for now, I dip my brush into a tub of shimmering black powder and smudge the color across my skin.

This is how I rid myself of the guilt.

This is how I try to understand.

The moment my mother's keys jangle in the front door, I toss her compacts back into her bag and sprint down the hall. I close and lock my bathroom door and twist the tub faucet on. Downstairs, my mother clicks on the TV. I throw my clothes to the floor in a wrinkled ball. The smell of gravy and meatloaf seeps through the ceiling vents. I inhale the familiar scent, lean against the ceramic countertop and stare into the fogged mirror at my naked self.

When the tub is filled, I slide in and let the steam melt the makeup from my face. Blackened drips of imaginary pain leave ripples on the water's surface. I submerge my head and open my eyes. Through the blur of the water, I watch as the colors of my fake sadness disappear into the heat.

I want to remember the first time we met.

I search my mind and struggle to find that initial memory. A vision of us on the blacktop. A memory of a schoolyard romp. An image of her and me in our party dresses and white fold-over socks. I crave the opportunity to, if only for a second, breathe in her childhood smell: that sticky, grass-stains-on-your-knees, sugary-cereal-on-your-breath scent of being so young.

I want to close my eyes and see a clear vision of her face, at age five or six, when her expressions were carefree, and her only stain a smear of ginger freckles spread across her skin. To reach out my palm and feel her tiny hand press against mine. To wrap my whole self around her and protect her from all the things I never could towards the end.

I want to remember what it was like before the sickness came. Before it took over her face and her mind and my heart.

But more importantly, I want to come to terms with this fact: that many of my most important memories — the moments that defined who she was, the ones that define who I become more each day — have slipped through the cracks in my mind.

And just like dust, just like her body that once stood before me, they have blown away, and are gone.

Kelsey and I are alone in her bedroom. We are surrounded by the darkness of the night sky. The darkness of the eggplant walls. The darkness that has become her constant mood. We sit on her bed, plush comforters draped across our shoulders, and balance bowls of Neapolitan ice cream in our laps. We are about sixteen.

I lick a thin layer of chocolate from my spoon and suggest we retreat to the den to watch TV. Kelsey shakes her head.

"Can we just talk for a while?" she asks.

Kelsey and I talk frequently, about little things, about big things, about the in-between things that make up day-to-day life. Rarely does she make it a point to request these sorts of conversations, as they tend to come to us naturally. When she does, I know something specific is on her mind.

A light rain taps the window. I pull the blanket closer to my neck.

"What's up?" I say and lift my spoon to my mouth.

Kelsey's expressions have grown increasingly solemn over the past few months. It is as though all the muscle has been drained from her body and has been replaced with a foreign, lifeless liquid instead. The skin on her face hangs from her bones, void of emotion. Rarely does it move to form a smile of excitement; rarely does it wrinkle with the joy of a laugh.

"Where do you think we go," Kelsey says, "when we die?"

I swirl my spoon in my bowl and mix the defined flavors into a mud-colored puddle.

"To our own version of heaven," I say.

Kelsey wraps the blanket over her head and around her chin like a babushka, presses her back against the wall, and sighs. She stares ahead of her. Our eyes don't meet.

"Do you ever think about your wake?" she says. "About who will come. Or about what they will say."

"Sometimes," I say. "Sometimes, when I'm really sad, I do."

"Me too," she says and pulls the blanket taut around her hairline.

I rest my face on Kelsey's shoulder, breathe deep, and absorb her scent. Kelsey rests her cheek against my head. She tells me she fears that, when her time comes, people will act out of line. She names friends and rattles off the actions she is certain they will take. So and so will throw herself across the casket, screaming and crying for everyone to see. Another friend will use the event as an excuse to sob on the shoulder of an attractive boy. Another will be too busy to show up at all.

"I know how our friends can be," she says. "They'll try to steal the spotlight from me."

I nod and silently understand.

"If I ever go before you," she says, "just promise me that you'll be there, beside me, the whole time. Then neither of us will have to go through it alone."

"I'll make sure the spotlight is on you," I say.

We both remain silent and concentrate on the gentle rhythm of the rain.

"Why all the sad talk, anyway?" I say.

"I don't know," Kelsey says. "I just feel so...*trapped* lately."

As Kelsey speaks, I preoccupy myself with my ice cream. I never take a moment to ask her what she means.

Kelsey sets her bowl on a desk beside her bed. She suggests we watch a movie, something light to help lift the mood. As she steps into the hall, she clicks off her bedside lamp. On my way from the room, I pause at the window to study the white glow of streetlamps through the fat splatters of rain. The drops pour down the pane, making it difficult to distinguish shapes on the street just feet from where I stand. I observe my reflection, the transparent image of my face that is aligned with the drips that rush down the glass. For a moment, I feel like a prisoner, confined behind the weight of the rain.

Several years from now, on the day of Kelsey's wake, I will remember this night. For hours, I will sit in a chair directly across from where she lies, and stare at the bloated, vacant quality of her face. People will walk past in droves. Some will stop to politely shake my hand. Some will, in a dramatic gesture, throw their arms around my neck and press their fingers to my cheek. Some will rush past without saying anything at all. For hours, I will remain seated just feet from my friend's body, my palms pressed against my chair's cool metal frame as I observe her:

The caked makeup that covers her face.

Her pale hands, neatly folded across her chest.

The straight, lifeless smile that occupies her lips.

I will close my eyes and imagine that she is animated and seated at my side. In the distance, I will believe I hear the whisper of rain.

Here is what I wish I remembered:

A vision of Kelsey's body in a sterile hospital bed. Taupe colored straps clasped firmly at her ankles and her wrists. The streak of a single tear on her face.

To know what she looked like during the days and weeks she was locked away.

Here is what I do remember:

My mother interrupting my homework to pass me the cordless phone. Kelsey's mother on the other end. Learning that it happened again. Kelsey's collect phone calls every evening. The middle-aged schizophrenic who stood beside the payphone and repeated Kelsey's words into the receiver. Kelsey and I dubbing this woman the "parrot lady" and forcing laughter at this inside joke.

Wishing the hospital staff would allow me to visit Kelsey, just once. Knowing that, even if they had, I would have been too afraid to go.

Here is what I do not remember, the things I failed to ever say:

Mentioning the unmentionable: *Why did you try to kill yourself again? Why are you locked up again? Why have they taken you away from me again?*

Letting her know her sickness hurt me, too.

I remember the very first time. I rushed to Kelsey's house straight from school on the day she was scheduled to come home, my thoughts stuck somewhere between fear and humor as I absorbed the idea of what a jokester my friend was: actually attempting to take her life in order to skip a few days of school. Genius.

Only, when I arrived at Kelsey's house and let myself in with the key her mother left me in the mailbox, nothing seemed funny at all. The silence of the place was deafening.

The phone rang. Her mother called to tell me about some new

ground rules. I was no longer permitted to speak of things that might provoke a sense of jealously in Kelsey. Things like boyfriends, school dances, and Friday night plans. I remember her mother seemed so serious. I wanted to ask her if she got the joke. Through the phone, I heard her choke back sobs.

That afternoon, when Kelsey walked through the door, her face was drowned in defeat. She clicked on the kitchen-ceiling fan and moved towards the window. Without thinking much about it, she reached for her mother's pack of smokes that lay on the countertop and, for the first time, sparked the tip of a cigarette within her mother's view. Kelsey's mother and I watched Kelsey's hand rise and fall to her lips, mesmerized by the cloud of blue-gray smoke that streamed from her mouth. As the smoke thinned into a veil of fog, I reflected on all the years Kelsey and I cleverly cupped cigarettes in our palms. I could feel my own face becoming drowned in defeat. With the flick of a lighter, Kelsey took the first of many steps to uncover our years of secrets. She stared at me as she sucked back a long, slow drag. I studied her hand as it floated back and forth to her lips and wondered why she was betraying me. I wondered why, before her mother's eyes, she wanted to expose a hidden side of us both.

Kelsey's mother paused, momentarily stunned, and then, after just a few seconds, playfully rested her hand on her hip.

"What the hell?" she said through a smirk and reached for a cigarette of her own. She wrapped her lips tight around its filter, looked inquisitively into the haze of smoke that floated before her face, and then tossed me her pack.

"I guess we've got bigger problems on our hands then you girls smoking," she said.

This comment, I do remember, scored a big laugh from each of us.

On a Saturday night when we are about seventeen, Kelsey and I decide to share a night out on the town. The evening begins in a diner with a group of my girlfriends who attend my high school. Cordially, the girls greet Kelsey, who, despite having met them on several occasions, offers only a forced smile before the group of us settles in a vinyl booth. Our waitress sets a plastic pitcher of soda on our table as the girls and I begin to chat about a particularly attractive boy in our grade. As we speak, Kelsey remains quiet; the only part of her body that makes a sound is her foot, which she anxiously taps against the diner's linoleum floor.

While seated across from Kelsey I cannot help but compare her to my classmates and myself, each of us classic and comfortable in our crewneck sweatshirts, our worn cardigans and faded jeans, our hair twisted back into messy ponytails and loose French braids. Kelsey's face, which is significantly bloated as a result of the multiple prescription pills she is now meant to swallow every morning and night, is masked in dark makeup, thick lines of black shadow and liner rimming her eyes. Her once vibrant red hair, which she recently cut into a drastic pixie cut, is gone. After one of her latest solo trips to the local beauty supply shop, Kelsey made the decision to dye her hair the darkest shade of black she could find. Now, both her hair color and her eye makeup create a dramatic contrast when set against her milky skin. It seems that ever since we first made the decision to color our hair a few years back, Kelsey has made a commitment to physically alter her appearance. In recent months, she has made frequent trips to Philadelphia with a group of girls who attend her high school in order to visit a body art shop that caters to underage teens. In addition to the tattoos that now decorate her calves and the back of her neck, thin metal rods jut through her tongue, her eyebrow and her bottom lip. Although I do not dare to admit it aloud, Kelsey's new look sometimes makes her appear like a complete stranger to me. Both externally and internally, she has become so far removed from the person I knew when I was a kid.

When only crumbs remain, the other girls depart in order to get their beauty rest. In the parking lot, Kelsey and I debate calling it a night too before she convinces me to join her at a house party that is being thrown on the opposite end of town by a group of peers who attended our middle school and who now attend Kelsey's high school.

"Don't you want to see everyone?" she asks when I initially decline her offer. "Don't you miss them?"

I'm not certain if I do, in fact, miss them at all. But I miss Kelsey. She pouts her pierced lip and then smiles wildly when she sees me roll my eyes as I begin to give in to her request. Outside the diner I find a payphone booth and dial my home number. My mother, her voice already raspy from sleep, answers the phone. I explain that I plan to stay at Kelsey's house for the night and that I'll be home in the morning. She poses a few standard parental questions in regards to our intentions for the evening before Kelsey steals the phone from my hand.

"Don't worry," Kelsey says into the receiver. "You know she's safe with me."

Inside the party, girls sweat mascara down their cheeks, rock music blares from speakers, cigarettes are flicked and stomped out on the floor. I dance my way into the kitchen, squeeze through a wall of bodies, and join a group of former acquaintances for a round of shots. A boy with green, candy-colored hair, whom I hardly know, tosses me a can of piss warm beer and a flirtatious smile. I crack the top, suck off the foam, and return the smile, satisfied by the boy's gesture of teenage chivalry.

In another room, people are spread across the floor. I join their circle, wrap my lips around a small wooden pipe and blow the sweetly-fragranced smoke into the air; it floats in a spiral before it blends into the haze. Kelsey sits beside a boy I have never seen before. She leans close to his body and cuffs one of her pant legs to reveal her most recent body art: a brightly colored tattoo that spreads across the width of her shin.

"They're all symbols of luck," Kelsey says and seductively traces her finger across her skin.

"Why luck?" the boy says and touches his shoulder to hers. "You don't seem like the type of girl who needs any of that."

Kelsey flicks her tongue across the metal ring that hugs her bottom lip and touches her now inch-long black hair.

"I guess we all need a little extra from time to time," she says.

The pipe travels across the room and soon it feels as though we are all drifting inside a cloud. My eyelids flutter as my body becomes relaxed. But just as I rest my head against the floor and stare at the ceiling with a sense of ease, I hear it: the tapping. *Tap. Tap. Tap.* Before I sit up, I know where the sound comes from. I know when I look at Kelsey, her foot or her hand or her entire leg will be tapping a nervous rhythm that is out of her control. I scroll my eyes across the room and study her. Her fingers drum anxiously across her knee. Her foot repeatedly slaps the floor. I move my gaze back up her body and search for other signs. Her eyes have already taken on an absent stare. Her smile has vanished. I contemplate rushing from the room to avoid the whole mess I know is only seconds away. But I don't have the courage for that. And so, instead, I wait like some deranged newscaster who stands in the eye of the storm. *Tap. Tap.* It is only seconds until Kelsey leaps up, triggered by an invisible internal explosion.

And just like that, just like a gust of winter wind, she blows right through the room. That is how things work these days. One minute, she is here beside me, and in just seconds, she is gone.

I wait a few minutes before I go find her. I've learned this is the best strategy, the only strategy, really. It is best for us both that she lets some of her emotion blow out to sea. When I find Kelsey, she is alone, seated in her car. The interior light clicks on as I crawl inside. Her makeup runs down her cheeks like two glittered, black streams that she allows to drip onto her chest, though this isn't the part that worries me. The crying is like second nature at this point, something I've come to expect almost daily. What bothers me is the tapping. It is like a Richter scale for me to judge each of her quakes upon. But I know the drill. I light two cigarettes, place one between her lips and let the other rest between my fingers. I watch her thigh bounce up and down. And then I wait for her to begin.

"I don't know," she says. "I don't fucking know why you made me come here. I was fine, everything was fine, and then everyone puts all this pressure on me, you know?"

I don't know, but I nod anyway. I tap my cigarette against the edge of the window and carefully weigh my words before I speak.

"What did you take today?" I say in my most tiny voice. At this point, almost anything can cause her to erupt, and so I've learned to delicately dance across eggshells.

"What are you, the drug Nazi?" she says and slaps her hand against the steering wheel. "Or my doctor?" The speed of her hand increases. "Fuck you," she says and hits her hand, hard, against the dash. The tears spill from her like rain.

I try to remember that this moment will pass. That this is not my friend who speaks to me, but something else I will never truly understand.

"Did you take your pills today, Kelsey?" I say.

She flips down the visor mirror and stares into the blankness of her own bloodshot eyes. I wonder if she recognizes this change in her behavior, too. For a moment, she is quiet while she takes in the sight of her reflection. Her thigh slows to a gentle rock. She runs her fingers through her hair and dabs at the smeared makeup beneath her lashes.

"No," she says.

The car becomes so quiet that I hear the sound of our breath.

"I'll take a few in the morning though," she says and closes the mirror.

She twists the radio knob to a jazz station. The rat-tat-tat sounds fill the car and our silence. Kelsey's face has softened. The worst is over for now.

"You want to go for a drive or something?" she asks, her entire demeanor different than it was just seconds ago. "We can drive out to the park or something," she says. "Like when we were kids."

Opportunities like this — occasions for us to be alone together, to escape together — aren't frequent these days, and so I say, "Yes, that would be nice," even though I know neither of us is in any condition to drive. Without speaking another word, we turn the radio up to its highest notch, fold down the top of her red convertible, and, dismissing our drunkenness, swerve our way across town.

Kelsey parks the car in a field of grass and allows the headlights to shine across goalposts and bleachers. Barefoot, we dance to the whiny brass melody, spin in fast circles beneath the midnight sky, and then collapse to the ground. We run across the field and feel the breeze press against our skin. Our bodies stretched across the warm car hood, we talk about the sort of nothingness that means everything. We pass a flask of whiskey and laugh so hard that tears stream down our faces. Kelsey interlaces her hands with mine. Above us, the stars twinkle like neon. We wish we could lay here like this forever.

Back at the house, shots of Jack Daniels are handed to us upon our entry. The room begins to spin and in the blur I find myself upstairs with the green-haired boy and Kelsey. The boy's room is decorated with rock posters and crates of vinyl. Kelsey and I lay across the floor while the boy hangs his head upside down from the edge of the bed. We all sing along in unison to a track that blares from the stereo. When the song ends, Kelsey leaves the room.

Morning. A noise in the hall wakes me. I part my eyes into narrow slits, and find the sun peeks through slivers in the window shades. The boy's arm is tightly wrapped around my torso. I pull myself up, readjust my twisted t-shirt, and finger comb my hair. The boy feels my movements and whispers, "No. Stay." By the time I slide on my shoes and reach the door, his breath is heavy with sleep once more.

I stumble down the hallway and balance my body against a wall for support. The world feels brighter than usual this morning. My body feels weak. A girl from Kelsey's high school is spread across the floor, her brunette hair hanging loosely across her face.

"You seen Kel?" I say and shake the girl's leg with my foot.

Like a rag doll, the girl throws up her arm and, without ever lifting her head, points to a door at the end of the hall.

The room is illuminated by the purplish glow of black light. Bodies sit cross-legged on the carpet. They all pat their noses when I creak the door open. A boy with shoulder-length black hair scrapes a thin snowy line together across a plastic CD case and tells me that Kelsey was with them, but didn't look so good, started to freak out, and left with some guy.

"Said they were going for a ride," he says and casually sucks the line up through his nose.

I slam shut the door, uncertain which disgusts me more: the behaviors I've witnessed or my own unwillingness to disassociate myself from these people.

Outside, the muted grayness of night has begun to burn into the goldenness of morning. When I reach Kelsey's parking spot, it is empty. Above me, a flock of crows perch on a telephone wire and scream out complaints about the new day.

I return to the house, shake the green-haired boy awake, and ask him to wait with me for Kelsey to come back.

"Please," I say and try to force a flirtatious smile.

I stand in front of him silently for what feels like days as he decides. He rubs his eyes, grunts some incoherent words and then follows me to the living room. We curl our bodies against one another. He passes me a thin joint. I rest my head on his chest. On the TV screen, John Cusack holds a stereo above his head and pronounces love.

The kitchen door slams open. Glasses and cans crash to the floor with a loud clatter. Kelsey stands amongst the mess, her pupils glazed, black circles dripping beneath her eyes. Her purse hangs limply from her elbow. She sways into the countertop, and, when she does, the prescription pills she refuses to take shake like maracas inside her bag. Kelsey stares at me while she dabs her hand across her sweating forehead, patting the spot where her blonde eyebrows used to be. But like so much of Kelsey, her brows, too, are gone, shaved off in one of her many moments of manic rage. She wipes her hand across her *sick* brows — the thin black penciled eyebrows she now draws on her face to replace the natural brows she shaved — and then studies the ebony smudges on her hand. She wipes her palms across her denim jacket, her gaze still set on my face, and mumbles that this is all my fault. The boy takes a final pull from the joint and then grinds it into a plastic ashtray. An amused smirk spreads across his face.

"That is so punk rock," he says and smiles.

I tell the boy that he is an idiot, a real idiot, and have him help me escort Kelsey onto the couch. She struggles at first, kicks and yells, and calls me names before she rests her head across my legs. All in one breath she tells me that she hates me, that she fucking hates me, that she's sorry, that she loves me, that she is sad. I stroke my fingers through her hair the way that mothers sometimes do, despite the fact that I am, in reality, still a child myself. Kelsey's eyes flutter like an infant's.

"What did you take tonight?" I say, unsure if her behavior is the result of recreational pills and powders, or the absence of the pills she is prescribed. She opens her eyes into two half-moons.

"You know what we need?" she whispers, ignoring my question. She wraps her finger around the hem of my t-shirt. "Blackberry wine," she says, singing the phrase like the lyrics to a song.

"We can't go out there now," I say. "It's too late."

Kelsey buries her head in my lap.

"You know we'll never get to go," she says through a pout.

"Why do you do this to me?" I whisper, uncertain if I even want her to hear my words.

But she does hear them.

"Because you hate me," she says.

"That's not fair," I shout at her. "What you're doing to me is not fair. This isn't how normal friends act. My other friends don't act this way."

Guilt pulsates through my body because I know, although I don't want to admit, that she can't control these things. That her sickness is beginning to fully take over her body and her mind. But I've reached my breaking point. The anger spews from me.

"I just want you to be normal so that I can be normal for once. Do you realize you're fucking up my life, too? Why can't you just pull it together and act like everyone else? Why can't you just not be sad and instead do normal things with me? Why can't you just be a *normal* friend?"

The boy presses a pipe to his lips and looks at us through glassy eyes. Kelsey continues to ignore me and sings in a raspy, hushed voice.

121

Blackkkberryyy Wiiiiine. As she sings, her eyes begin to appear distant, like they are sinking someplace inside her skull. I stare into her face, into her drifting eyes, and see nothing. Once again, she has left me to wander the secret corridors of her mind. But before I can fully register this thought, Kelsey's jaw drops. The shrill sound of her scream competes with the quiet chime of church bells in the distance.

When Kelsey's scream ceases, she moves her lips in such a way that suggest she will speak. I pray she will say something significant. I pray she will provide me with the answers I so desperately need.

"Have you heard anything I've said?" I ask.

Kelsey looks at my face and smacks her tongue against the roof of her mouth.

"I need something to drink," is all she says.

Sunday morning. Cars are on the road, newspapers are being delivered, families are cooking breakfasts in their homes. I walk in the direction of a nearby convenience store but find myself moving towards a detour instead. I watch as cars trickle into the church parking lot — the same church where Kelsey and I attended catechism classes as kids. Mothers smooth their skirts as they step from their cars. Children wear miniature dresses and suits and chase one another up the church steps. Tears escape me while I witness their innocent faces explode with laughter. I close my eyes and say a brief prayer. *Please, God, let them always stay this carefree*. I move through the lot and press my face against the glass entrance to the building. Many of the pews remain empty. Rays of sunlight illuminate a wall of stained glass. Before I have a chance to process my actions, my body slides past the front door. My damp fingers press against my forehead and begin to make the sign of the cross. The holy water feels cool against my skin. *Help us*, I whisper and then disappear out a side door.

I open the glass door of the convenience store and am confronted with a wave of cool air. Goosebumps spread across my skin. Middle-aged men, who wear Dockers and baseball caps, wander the aisles. They purchase gallons of milk and eggs. I imagine them bringing their purchases home to their wives and children. For a second, I close my eyes and pretend I am at my own kitchen table, innocently blowing bubbles into a glass of chocolate milk. I lift my head, hoping to see the familiar scene of my home. Situated in front of me is a dusty display of sunflower seeds.

I look down at my body. The shape of my triangular breasts is evident beneath my paper-thin t-shirt. I ball the sleeves of my sky-blue cardigan, a recent gift from my mother, into my palms. I want so badly to appear like a normal teenage girl, just like one of my new high school friends, but I know I do not. My new wardrobe is only a façade. I touch my face. The dark eyeliner Kelsey used to line my eyes while we sat on her car hood is smeared like charcoal beneath my bottom lashes. One of the men observes me. My eyes begin to tear. I turn my head away from him and, when I do, catch a whiff of the stale, cigarette scent that lingers in my hair. In this moment, I wish I could collapse into the arms of this man. I want so badly to create an excuse. To tell him I am not the raggedy girl he sees. To tell him that my friend is sick and is getting worse every day. I want to tell him that I don't understand her diagnosis, and therefore, do not understand any potential cures. To tell him that I pray each night — for her and for me — my knees pressed hard against the carpet.

But I know he won't believe me.

And so, like so many other times in my life, I remain silent. Rather than speak the words that bubble on my lips, I skim the aisles and allow my skin to absorb the man's judgmental stares. I open the door of a cooler and trace my fingers across a chilled bottle of juice. I look back at the man. I want to look him in the eye and hope he will understand.

Before our gazes have the opportunity to meet, my mind becomes consumed with an image of Kelsey's face. I grip the drink in my hand. Right now, this perspiring, two-dollar bottle is the only cure I comprehend. This is the only way I know how to help save her.

At the counter, I drop an armful of gummy bears, Gatorade and cigarettes beside the register and wipe the tears that flood my eyes. The Indian clerk looks at me and smiles. Despite his quiet demeanor, I know he savors the satisfaction of this moment. I know he enjoys seeing that the girl who, for so many years, came into his store with her red-headed friend to steal Slurpees and smokes, the girl who once childishly mocked his cloth turban, has ended up here, reeking of booze and cigarettes on a Sunday morning. He places my items into a plastic bag.

"Thank you," he says in his thick accent and I know that he means it.


When I return, Kelsey and the boy are asleep beside one another on the couch. I softly shake Kelsey and uncap a drink. Her shoulders jerk.

"Blackberry wine?" she says and smiles in an optimistic, childlike sort of way.

"No, Kel," I say. "It's eight a.m. on a Sunday. That place isn't even open right now."

She sloppily chews a green gummy worm and lights a smoke.

"You hate me," she says and sighs dramatically.

"Please stop, Kel. I don't hate you," I say.

I try to run my fingers across her face. She pushes my hand away.

"How did we get here?" I whisper and allow tears to flow down the skin of my face.

Kelsey kicks the boy in his thigh.

"She hates me," she says. "She fucking hates me."

The boy squints and pulls on the thick, black eyeglasses that have fallen into his lap. He looks at Kelsey and then at me.

"That is so punk rock," he says, tilts his head, and closes his eyes once more.

One night, just a few weeks before her eighteenth birthday, Kelsey goes to sleep. And in the morning, she does not want to get out of bed.

Kelsey's emotional state has become a sort of seesaw. Some mornings she wakes and is perfectly fine, happy to step away from her bed and out into the world. But on other days, on the bad days, just the thought of having to leave her bed is enough to paralyze her. Hidden beneath mountains of plush quilts and thick layers of down, Kelsey sometimes stays in bed for entire days, interspersed between cycles of sleeping and silently staring at the black and blue walls that surround her.

When this first begins, I frequently remind myself that Kelsey suffers from the flu (despite the fact that she never coughs, never sneezes, and never expresses that she actually has a flu at all), and therefore rationalize her sleeping until ten o'clock, eleven o'clock, or noon on many days. But after several weeks, I begin to notice that Kelsey's flu has not gone away and that the hours she spends in bed rapidly increase. Now, on some days, she conceals herself beneath her bed sheets until two o'clock, four o'clock, or seven o'clock in the evening. These are considered good days. On the bad days, she never leaves her bed at all.

Sometimes her parents will try to gently coax her. Other times, due to their own anger and fear, they will raise their voices and slam doors and make comments that suggest their daughter is lazy and not actually ill. Now and again, too exhausted to continue fighting against Kelsey's invisible sickness, they will simply close her bedroom door and try to ignore the fact that she has remained in bed for ten, twelve or fifteen hours on any given day. Trying to get Kelsey out of bed has become a sort of twisted game for us all.

"Hey, Kel. Look how beautiful it is outside today," I say on some days and slowly twist open her bedroom blinds. I gently tap her shoulder, though she does not budge. Rather, her focus remains on the ceiling, as though I am not here, standing beside her, at all.

"Hey, Kel. I made you breakfast. There's a plate waiting for you in the kitchen," I say on other days, swing open her bedroom door, and allow the scent of bacon to waft in behind me. Kelsey takes one look at me, sinks deeper into her bed, and scrunches her nose, sickened by the smell.

"Hey, Kel. I bought us tickets to a concert. Why don't you jump in the shower and we can go, okay?" I say on some weekend nights and wave the tickets in front of her face, knowing, even as I do, that she will not move. That instead, she will stare at the darkness of her walls and tightly clutch her blankets in her fists.

This is when I begin to beg.

"Hey, Kel. Can you please get out of bed today?" I say and shake her firmly by her arms. *"Because you haven't moved in days and I'm scared and I'm running out of steam and I don't know what else there is that's left for me to do."*

As I expect, my efforts end in defeat.

"Hey, Kel, you have to get out of bed today, because this place is a mess," I say. *"Because you are a mess, and I am becoming a mess as a result. Because I miss you and I do not understand what is going on inside your head. Because I need you to be here, living in the world, with me, and not curled up beneath your sheets. I need you to wake up, wake up, WAKE UP...please."*

On some rare days, Kelsey actually does leave her bed. She makes her way into the kitchen, though often, this is as far as she goes. Her lips are turned down, the skin beneath her eyes two heavy, sagging bags. She presses her waist against the counter. A cigarette dangles from her lips. For hours, she stands, speechless, and gazes out the window. On these days, I occasionally try to break the cold silence that stirs between us.

"Hey, Kel. Look how nice it is outside today. Why don't we take a drive? Maybe go some place and buy CDs," I say.

As I expect, Kelsey does not respond. Instead, she stubs out her cigarette, examines her prescription pillbox, skeptically eyeing the rainbow of pills — the silent killers — that live beneath its lid, and returns to her room.

In a matter of weeks, Kelsey has become a modern day Sleeping Beauty, her body bound to the confines of her bed. Sometimes, as she lies twisted in her sheets, stuck in a torturous sleep, I watch her and wonder about the person she used to be. I wonder if that person has entirely disappeared or if a piece of her is trapped inside this stranger beside me, fighting to break free.

I lean down and softly kiss Kelsey's cheek, hoping I have the power to end this evil spell. Hoping that the touch of my skin or the saltiness of my tears will be enough to save her. She parts her eyes into narrow slivers and reaches her arms towards me for what seems to be an embrace. *The curse has been shattered*, I think and my heart flutters with joy. *My friend has finally returned.*

But just as I begin to lower my body into Kelsey's arms, I notice she gazes at me with an unfamiliar sneer. It takes only seconds until her hands are pressed against me and then forcefully pushing me away. My body stumbles backwards for several feet. An emptiness grows in my belly as I stare into Kelsey's absent eyes. I wait for her to speak, expecting an explanation. There is only silence between us.

I regain my footing and press my fingers to the corners of my eyes. My lips part as I prepare to ask Kelsey for an answer. I need her to provide a reason for why she has changed.

But I am too slow.

Or maybe, in truth, I am too afraid.

In an instant, my Sleeping Beauty returns to her hibernation, and I return to my game.

"Hey, Kel. Would you like to take a walk and get some air? We can go sit down by the lake, like when we were kids," I whisper.

Only, she does not answer. She simply turns onto her side, her back to my face, a wall of blankets separating these two young women who, once upon a time, were friends.

*I could sit all day and all night inside this purple room.*

"Okay then, Kel. Maybe you'll feel more up to it tomorrow," I say and sit beside her on the bed, even though I am certain that, by tomorrow, nothing will change. Kelsey will stay in bed. And I, still so hopeful, will try to make her move.

To make her whole again.

Come tomorrow, Sleeping Beauty will go on with her never-ending sleep. I will go on playing my never-ending game. And the curse that has captured us both will control us this way forever.

One afternoon, after I coax her to leave her bed, Kelsey and I sit beside one another on her living room sofa and peer through the window shades. We both nervously tap our feet against the carpeting and bounce our hands on our thighs each time a car drives down the street.

"I'm so anxious to see who it is," I finally say.

"It's not going to be anyone that fabulous," Kelsey reassures me. "Teachers only do this to make a little extra side cash. It's probably just some lame teacher from another school."

"I wonder if it will be a teacher from my high school," I say.

"Look, you don't need to make such a big deal out of this," Kelsey says and lights a cigarette. "It's *just* school."

"You're right," I say. "It's crazy, though. I can't believe you don't have to go to school for the rest of senior year. I can't believe that a teacher is coming here — to your house — to teach you."

There is a knock at the front door. I sprint down the hall steps. Kelsey slowly moves behind me, a cigarette dangling from the corner of her mouth, and absently swings open the front door. A middle-aged man with unkempt hair and a stained tie waits for us on the porch.

"Well," the man says upon taking in the sight of Kelsey and me. "It seems some friendships never die."

"Mr. Anderson?" Kelsey says. "Why are *you* here? I thought they'd send someone from another district or something."

Mr. Anderson, our former eighth-grade math teacher and the former target of Kelsey's many teenage pranks, pushes his way past us, sets his briefcase on the kitchen table and unlatches a series of metal clasps.

"So, what sort of stunt did you girls pull this time?" he asks sarcastically.

"I'm the only one here being homeschooled. She didn't pull any stunts," Kelsey clarifies and nods in my direction. "She doesn't even go to school with me anymore."

"Interesting," Mr. Anderson says in a disinterested tone. He pulls an assortment of worksheets from his briefcase and spreads them across the table. "So, which of your antics landed you six months of home schooling?" he asks. "Drinking in school? Skipping school? Perhaps smoking in school?" he says and waves away a cloud of smoke that drifts from Kelsey's cigarette towards his face.

"I tried to kill myself," Kelsey says.

Mr. Anderson stares silently at Kelsey, clearly trying to determine the veracity of her statement.

"Those are all mine," Kelsey says and casually points towards a display of prescription pill bottles that line the countertop. "You can check the labels if you want. They all have my name on them. My doctors apparently think I'm crazy. Too crazy for school at least."

Mr. Anderson eyes the pill bottles and the emotionless void that is expressed on Kelsey's face. He mindlessly sorts through his papers in an effort to avoid making eye contact with her.

"When?" he asks.

"A bunch of times, actually. Turns out I'm not very good at it though," she says.

"So then you're done with school?" he asks, his tone suddenly suggesting concern.

"I'm not *done* with school," Kelsey says. "I'm still going to get my diploma. My doctors just don't think it's a good idea for me to actually *go* to school anymore. Too much pressure. Too much stress."

"You know, Kelsey," Mr. Anderson says and realigns his gaze with hers. "The last time I saw you was your last day of eighth grade. I believe you told me that you were 'glad you'd never have to see my fucking face again.'"

"Yeah, well, fate is a real bitch," Kelsey says and stubs out her cigarette.

Mr. Anderson absently taps his pen against his chin and momentarily loses himself in thought.

"Why are you here?" he says and looks at me.

I shrug.

"I don't know," I say. "I thought it'd be fun."

"You thought *this* would be fun?" he asks.

"Well, maybe not fun," I clarify. "I just felt like I needed to be here. I wanted to be here."

The truth is that I can't bear to miss a single minute when Kelsey is out of her bed.

"You can't be here," he instructs me. "If you really want to help your friend, go home and leave her alone so she can get her work done. Unless, of course, your goal is for her to *not* finish high school."

Kelsey looks to me in such a way that expresses a sense of agreement.

"I thought you wanted me here?" I say to Kelsey.

"I did. But, you know, maybe it will be better if you're not. I mean, you've already heard about all this stuff in your own math class anyway."

"I'll listen to it again if you want to hang out," I say, anxious to spend time with her — regardless of the specific activity — outside of her bedroom.

"Look. I have to get this stuff done. Just swing by when you leave school tomorrow," Kelsey tells me and escorts me towards the front door.

I spend the next hour walking around Kelsey's block, hoping each time I approach her house that she will be waiting for me on the front step.

But the door never opens.

I make my way towards the elementary school at the end of Kelsey's street and situate myself on a set of concrete steps. I watch groups of children as they run through the grass. They tumble onto the ground, dirtying themselves, before springing back up and twirling freely across the fields.

A pain grows inside me.

Before I have a chance to process the source of it, my chest heaves and my face and neck are damp from tears.

June. The last six months have been a blur. College guidance meetings. Proms. My first broken heart after my boyfriend, Brad, accepts a job offer on the west coast. And now this: my high school graduation.

My mother assists me as I drape my white graduation gown across my body. My father slides a white and silver corsage onto my wrist. Before we find our way to our final destination – my high school football field – we make a detour to Kelsey's home. I exit the car. Beams of humid sunlight beat down on me and instantly make the polyester gown stick to my skin. Kelsey's mother and father both greet me and express congratulatory words. While my parents and Kelsey's parents engage in brief conversation, I move past the entryway in order to find Kelsey. She is curled on the sofa, her knees pressed against her chest, the shape of her body hidden beneath a bulky black wool sweater.

"Aren't you dying in that thing?" I ask and playfully tug on Kelsey's sleeve. "It's, like, a hundred degrees out."

"I'm fine," she says.

In the next room, Kelsey's black graduation gown is draped across a dining room chair.

"Are you going to go?" I ask when she catches me staring at it.

"I don't know yet," she says and lights the tip of a cigarette. She is quiet for a moment as she enjoys her smoke.

"Days like this make me wish we had gone to high school together," Kelsey finally says. "Today would have been a lot different if we had."

It hurts me to know that Kelsey is more than likely right. Perhaps if we had attended the same high school things would have ended differently. But differently for who? For her? For me? For us both?

"Seriously, though," I say in an effort to change the topic. "They picked the hottest day of the year for this. I'm going to be sweating through my gown the whole time and – "

"You'll love every minute of it," Kelsey says. "You look really nice

132

by the way."

"I do?" I say and self-consciously comb my fingers through my hair. "Thanks, Kel. That means a lot."

Our parents enter the living room. Kelsey's parents each pour celebratory glasses of blush wine. My mother snaps pictures of every person in the room. She asks Kelsey and me to pose. I stand behind Kelsey, prop my head on her shoulder and wrap my arms around her waist; when I do, the armholes of my white gown drape in such a way that, later, when I look at the photograph, they will look like a pair of wings.

After the picture has been snapped Kelsey takes hold of my right hand.

"You wore your ring," she points out.

"Of course I did," I say. "I told you I'd wear it everyday."

Last week, I arrived at Kelsey's house at the end of a long school day. When I walked inside I found her seated and waiting for me on a living room armchair, a small wrapped box resting on her lap.

"What's that?" I asked. "My birthday isn't until August, you know?"

"It's a graduation gift," she said and handed the box to me.

Carefully, I unwrapped the metallic paper and opened the small velvet box.

"Best friend charms aren't my style," Kelsey said as I stared at the smooth silver band. "The truth is that I know that one day you'll find someone to replace me. You'll find your real soul mate who will give you some really fancy ring. But I don't care about that. To me, you're my soul mate. And so I wanted to give you a ring, too."

As I pulled the ring from the box I caught a glimpse of the engraving on the inside of the simple silver band.

*Friends Forever, 2000.*

"It's perfect," I told her and slid the ring onto my right ring finger. "It's the best thing you've ever given me."

"So then you'll wear it?" she asked.

"Everyday," I told her. "Everyday from now until forever."

"Good," Kelsey said and pulled another silver band from her pant pocket. "This one is identical to yours," she said. "Same band. Same engraving. Only this one is for me."

Kelsey slid her ring onto her finger. "If we both promise to wear them everyday," she said, "then even when we're away from each other, it will seem like we're never really apart."

My mother snaps a few final photos and then checks her watch. It's time.

"I'm really proud of you," Kelsey whispers to me as I find my way towards the door. "You're going to do a lot of great things."

"I'll call you after the ceremony," I tell her, though once I get caught up in the graduation festivities, I never do.

Later that afternoon, as I sit among a sea of white gowns, I slip my foot from my heeled sandal and twirl my toes around blades of dry grass. My name is called. I slide on my sandal and walk towards the podium, pausing long enough for my mother to snap a photo of me as I receive my diploma. By the time I arrive back at my seat, excitement builds amongst my peers. The administrators are nearing the name of the final graduate. Soon, we all wildly toss our crisp white graduation caps into the air. I tilt up my head and watch as my cap somersaults towards the clouds and then momentarily disappears in a beam of golden sunlight. I hold my hand to my forehead in an effort to block out the sun. As I do the sun glints off my ring. The sight of twinkling metal possesses me. For a moment I forget where I'm at and why I'm there. All I can concentrate on is the ring and the thought of Kelsey's words. *It will seem like we're never really apart.* Something brushes my foot. I glance down and see that my cap has fallen and landed on my polished toes. I shake my foot and watch as the cap briefly launches back in the air before it floats in a final trip towards the ground.

Upon completing high school I speak with my parents and ultimately make the decision to stay home for one more year. They are not thrilled with my choice, though they seem to understand.

When people ask me why I've decided to take courses at the local community college for my first two semesters I offer them a string of lies. *It's a smart financial decision. I can experiment with different liberal arts courses. My parents need my help around the house with some things.*

The truth is that I'm terrified to leave her.

The following spring I find myself in a cheap hotel room drinking with Kelsey and a group of friends. Kelsey lethargically sits on the bed and leans her back against the headboard while the rest of us dance across the carpeting. My cell phone rings. My mother tells me that she just checked the mail and then begs me to allow her to open the large envelope that arrived. I hear her slice through the paper just before she screams her joy through the line.

I click shut my phone.

"I got in," I exclaim. "I'm moving to Vermont this fall!"

Several friends rush to me and wrap their arms around my body. Kelsey remains seated on the bed, a can of beer in her hand.

Several weeks after my acceptance letter arrives, my parents invite Kelsey to join us on a weekend trip to Vermont so that we can all get a better feel for the town I will soon call home. My sister, who is in her mid-twenties, is occupied with her own adult life and thus there is an extra seat available in my parents' car. Kelsey has recently started taking a few new medications, which have helped her to regain some of her energy and motivation for life. She has even picked up a part-time job at a local coffee shop.

When we arrive in Vermont, we eat homemade chowder at a waterfront restaurant. We walk through the downtown and meander in and out of the many bohemian shops. We browse apartment listings and try to imagine where I will store all of my clothes and books.

Kelsey and I are in the backseat of my parents' car. My father listens to sports radio while my mother admires the passing scenery.

"I wish I could move up here with you," Kelsey whispers to me. "This town is so cool. It's so different from back home."

"So do it. Move here with me," I say. "We can get a two-bedroom. You can get a job downtown somewhere."

"I'd love that," she says.

"Then do it," I say.

"I don't think I'll be allowed," she says and busies her mind by staring out the window. I'm not certain who she believes will restrain her: her doctors, her parents, or herself.

"But you'll come visit me, won't you?" I ask after a moment of silence.

"It's too far," she says and she is right to say so. Whether I did so consciously or not, I've chosen a school that is a seven-hour drive away from her.

"Mom," I say and lean closer to the front seat. "Didn't you say there is a train line that runs from New Jersey to someplace nearby campus?"

"Yup," my mother says, still smitten by the quaintness of the town. "And Kelsey knows she can drive up here with us anytime she'd like."

I continue to skim the newspaper classifieds in search of two-bedroom listings.

"You're never going to come home from here," Kelsey finally says.

"Of course I will," I say. "I'll be home for Thanksgiving and for Christmas and —"

"No," she says. "I mean that you're never really going to live at home again. You'll never want to leave this place. You'll never come back to our town."

"I'm sorry," I whisper so that my parents won't hear.

"Don't be," she says. "You belong in a place like this. I wish I did, too."

For months now, Kelsey and I have been separated by vast stretches of winding highway. I am a college freshman, studying at a school several states from my home, in a small town that is far from my family, far from my friends, and far away from her.

Since being at college, I have become overwhelmed by a strange sense of relief. I'm not exactly certain what I feel relief from. However, I know I feel it most when surrounded by my new college friends. These friends spend hours fondly recalling childhood memories of their sheltered New England hometowns; they still choke when they sip warm, watery beer; with innocent enthusiasm, my new friends recall stories of summer camps and school pep rallies and all the other things I seem to have missed. And for these things, I admire them.

I admire that none of my new friends talk about hospital bracelets, or prescription pills, or snaking lines of scab that run across their flesh. My new friends listen to Van Morrison records and swipe bone-colored polish across their nails. Together, we spend lazy afternoons shopping for peasant blouses and tortoise shell hair clips and eating Indian cuisine. On Friday nights, my new friends do not call me from the payphone in a psychiatric ward. Rather, they lay with me, barefoot, on the campus green, to sip wine coolers and study the stars.

Some nights, while my toes are curled around damp blades of grass, I think of her. In my mind, I create scenarios of how things might change if she were here with me now. I think about how different life would be if she were not a sick girl. Would our friendship still be the same? Would I still be the same? I think about how much her illness has actually impacted both our lives. But I could never share these thoughts with Kelsey, because she would never understand. She is too *sick* to comprehend what I mean. And so, instead, I run my fingers through the grass and silently appreciate the sense of normalcy my new friends bring to my life. But more, I appreciate the sense of normalcy they bring out in me.

December. The fall semester is rapidly coming to an end. In recent weeks, books and essays and final exams have begun to consume me. It is during this already stressful time that Kelsey decides to call with more frequency. Sometimes, she calls in the early morning while I am still curled in my sheets. Other times, she calls late in the evening and wakes my roommate and me. Though Kelsey never says so directly, I can tell by the tone of her voice that something is wrong. That there is something she is not telling me. And for the first time since leaving home, I begin to feel guilty for choosing a school that is so far away. For creating such distance between us during the time I know she needs me most.

My roommate and I are sprawled across the floor of our dorm room amongst piles of note cards and books when the phone rings.

"Hey. It's me," Kelsey says, and her voice sounds somehow small.

"Hi," I say. "Look, I can't really talk for long. I've got this exam tomorrow and —"

"I just wanted to tell you that I miss you," she whispers.

"Oh. I miss you, too," I say, ashamed for trying to rush her off the line. "Is everything okay back home?"

"Yeah. Everything is fine," Kelsey says and pauses briefly. "I just wanted to know if you want to go for a drive."

I press my hand against the receiver and ask my roommate for some privacy. The door quietly clicks shut behind her.

"Where are you, Kel?" I say.

"At home. In bed," she says softly.

"Is anyone else there with you?" I say.

"My parents are in the living room, I think," she says.

"Did something happen?" I say.

"No. I just want us to go for a drive," she says, as though the fact that I am more than three-hundred and fifty miles away from her is not a factor.

"Kelsey," I say. "You know we can't go for a drive tonight. I'm too far away."

Kelsey sighs.

"I knew you'd say that," she says.

"But I promise that as soon as I get home for Christmas, the first thing we will do together is take a long drive someplace, okay?" I say.

"I want to go for a drive with you right now and sing," she says. "We can roll the windows down and turn the music up like it is summer. We can drive down to the ocean."

"That sounds really nice," I say and realize my neck is damp with tears. "I swear, as soon as I get home, Kel, that's what we'll do. Just you and me, okay?"

"Can we sing together now?" she says. "Just for a minute."

Kelsey promises to crawl from her bed and put on our favorite CD. Several states away, I turn my dorm room stereo onto the same track.

"Will you dance with me, too?" she says.

I close my eyes and try to become lost in the sounds of the song. My feet twirl around stacks of textbooks and I imagine Kelsey doing the same. I concentrate on her voice as she sings the lyrics to me and think back to when we were young — so many moments that I sat and listened to her sing, her voice ricocheting off tiled walls. A stream of tears slides down my cheeks as I envision Kelsey the way she was back then. In my daydream, our hands are interlaced as we spin in fast circles. Her body feels weightless and alive. She glows a healthy glow. A sincere smile is spread across her face.

The door swings open. My eyes bolt wide and glance at my roommate in the doorframe, a pile of books resting in her arms.

"Are you almost done in here?" she says and, before I can answer, begins to resettle her body onto the floor.

I move to the opposite end of the room, my back to my roommate so she cannot see my reddened face.

"Look, Kel," I whisper. "I have to run, okay? But I'll be home next week and we can sing more then."

"I really need you to be here right now, though," Kelsey says and as she does, I hear the crinkling of her sheets through the line.

In my heart, I know Kelsey has not moved since our conversation began. I know that, right now, a mound of blankets covers her body. But

I try to push this thought away. I try to push everything away. Instead, I force myself to think of her when she was well.

"I know you do," I say. "I'll be home soon."

In my head, I can see the smile she once wore so well and hear the tone of her voice before the sickness came and stole it away.

"I really need you here to help make all this go away," she says.

I close my eyes and envision her as a young teenager, dancing. Her arms are thrown above her head. Her mouth is sprung open in a wide grin. Tiny, strawberry blonde braids fall and frame her face. And with this thought, all the images I have archived in my brain — all the images of her as a sick girl — momentarily fade away.

"I just really need you to come home."

Why, God, can I not remember? I squeeze my eyes shut and try to summon the memory. Was it on the school playground, where we ran across steaming, September pavement? Was it her birthday party? The one where her mother sat in an armchair, clutching a glass of blush wine, and I, afraid of a clown, crouched behind a grandfather clock all afternoon?

I want to remember that first instant. That initial "hello." Our original moment of play. I want to pinpoint it and determine if anything seemed wrong back then. To conclude if the sickness was always inside her, hibernating, or if it was planted and sowed at some point further down the line.

At times, I have become jealous of my own mother as she describes, with accurate detail, her first memory of Kelsey. It was the morning of my sixth birthday. I woke early, slipped into my blue party dress, and sat anxiously at the edge of our drive. One by one, my classmates arrived on our doorstep, handed my mother fancily wrapped gifts and skipped inside. I followed them indoors and waited beside the front window for Kelsey to arrive. When she did, she tapped on our screen door, dutifully handed my mother a beribboned box and, in her six-year old voice, said that her parents despised our neighborhood.

"It ruined all the cornfields," Kelsey said, turned around, and proudly waved to her mother as her car backed onto the street.

My mother and Kelsey grew close as the years passed. It became common for me to come home from high school and find the two of them seated in our living room drinking tea. For a period, it became normal for Kelsey to turn up on our doorstep after a fight at home, a duffel bag hung from her shoulder, in search of someplace to run away to for a night, a week, a month. My mother learned never to ask Kelsey about the argument. Rather, she pulled out an extra set of bed linens, and oversaw Kelsey's phone call to her own mother to inform her that she was staying someplace safe.

Not too long ago, I asked my mother for permission to open her wallet in order to make change for a large bill. As I fingered through the paper contents, I found a neatly folded, yellowed piece of loose leaf. Something urged me to unfold the note. I did, and found Kelsey's faded, bubbly cursive spread across the page.

"What the hell is this?" I said to my mother.

My mother sighed, as though embarrassed by my accidental find.

"Kelsey gave that note to me years ago, when you two were kids," my mother said. "You had both been caught drinking someplace, and she was afraid I'd never let her see you again. She wanted to make sure I knew you weren't the one to blame. She wanted to make sure I wasn't going to force you to stop being her friend."

Some days, when my efforts to remember our first meeting end in defeat, I am tempted to perch at the end of my drive — a little girl in my favorite blue dress — and wait to see if, somehow, she might still appear from around the bend.

Though I don't often like to admit it, I do believe she planned it all, right down to the last detail.

It is the week of Christmas and every face from our past is back on common ground. Friends have come from California, Boston, Florida, Manhattan and Philadelphia to visit family, friends, and each other.

In Kelsey's mind, we are all here for one final celebration. For one final goodbye.

Friends are crammed into a dirty dive bar placed smack in the center of our hometown. We gulp dollar beers beside the glow of flickering, neon advertisements. The night is filled with blurry laughter and gossip about new boyfriends, new classes, new dorm rooms, new lives. Kelsey chimes in and playfully describes her most recent hospital stay and the friendly hospital workers who took away all her pencils, zippers, safety pins, disposable razors, rubber bands, shoelaces, headbands, and bobby pins.

"Weapons of self-destruction," she says and roars with laughter.

And somehow, her laughter makes the whole mess of things seem okay. We all laugh along with Kelsey and raise a glass to her kind-hearted hospital staff. May they have a happy, healthy new year.

Somebody gets his hands on a camera and blue flashes spark throughout the smoky space, prompting exaggerated poses and wide, drunken grins. A familiar face stumbles towards me and I toss her my disposable cardboard camera. I stretch my arm around Kelsey's waist. She presses her cheek to mine. In my mind, the noise of the place fades to a muted buzz, and, for a split second, life begins to slow down. In this instant, all that exists is us — Kelsey and me — just like old times. Our hands clutch drinks. Our faces touch.

In this moment, life feels good again. Life feels as it should.

One.

Two.

Cheese.

The flash illuminates the darkened space. Weeks from now, when the film is developed, in the background of the photo, friends will appear like blurred, moving shadows amongst the reflections of neon signs. Kelsey's pale, bloated face will look soft from the rush of white light, her smile like a calm in the center of the otherwise bustling room.

It is the last photograph ever taken of her.

It is the week of Christmas and I am asleep in Kelsey's home. Kelsey wakes early. She hovers over my sleeping body, a smile spread across her freshly washed face.

"Good morning, sunshine," she says and twists open the blinds. Golden sunlight pours across the room.

"What time is it?" I say, my voice still raspy from sleep.

"It's early," she says and crawls beside me.

She rests her head against my shoulder.

"It's really nice out today," she says and leans toward the window.

"How long have you been awake?" I say, surprised she is up and out of bed at all.

"For a while," she says. "I couldn't sleep last night. I had a lot on my mind."

As I stretch my arms and release a muffled yawn, I try to imagine what thoughts could have prevented Kelsey from sleep. She speaks before I have a chance to ask.

"Can we spend the day together today?" she says. "Just us."

"Yeah, sure. Of course," I say, and, when I do, it occurs to me that Kelsey and I haven't spent a full afternoon alone together in months. "Is there somewhere special you want to go?" I ask.

She shakes her head.

"I don't care where we go really," she says. "I just want to spend the day together. Just me and you."

In minutes, we are bundled in wool caps and gloves. Icy clouds float from our lips. We listen as music buzzes through the speakers of the car.

Kelsey and I spend the next several hours driving without a sense of purpose or direction, talking about the sort of seemingly insignificant details that give life meaning. Each time we reach an intersection, Kelsey flips a quarter to determine whether I should turn the steering wheel left or right, less concerned with where we are heading then we are with the conversation coming to a close. By mid-afternoon, our quarter has led us down a series of wooded back roads, across bridges, under tollbooths, over highways, and onto an unfamiliar road in Pennsylvania. Kelsey twists down the volume knob on the radio.

"Look," she says. "I have to tell you something. But you're going to be pissed."

She takes a final drag from her cigarette and rolls up the window, eliminating the whistling sound of winter wind from the interior of the car.

"I stopped taking my medicine," she says without any hesitation.

"What do you mean you stopped?" I say. "Like, your doctor took you off them?"

"No," she says. "I've been weaning myself off them for a while."

"Do you mean you've been weaning yourself off a certain prescription?" I say, even though, in my heart, I am already certain of the answer. "Or — "

"I know it seems crazy," she says. "But I can't live my life like — "

"How long have you been doing this?" I say.

Kelsey turns to face the window. For a moment, she is silent. She studies the passing scene outside the glass.

"I haven't taken a pill in days," she says. "Maybe weeks. I'm not sure how long."

The car remains quiet for several minutes, the only sound the gentle rattle that rises from under the dash.

"Aren't you scared?" I say.

"Of what?" she says. "That I'll freak out or something."

I nod.

"A little," she says and turns to face me. "But the thing is, I feel great. I feel better than I have in a really long time. I think those pills are what are bad for me. I don't think there is anything wrong with me. I think it's just having that shit in my system all the time, you know?"

I nod again, though I am not certain I agree.

I know it is wrong for Kelsey to stop taking her pills. I know what the textbooks would say: that her body and her mind are bound to crash. That I should tell someone. That I should pull the car over, dig through her purse, and force the pills into her mouth myself. But the truth is that she does seem better.

Kelsey turns to me and smiles.

I think about how I've missed that smile so desperately.

I think about how, today, Kelsey's body is not twisted in bed sheets; instead, she is out here, in the world, with me. We've listened to music and screamed the lyrics out loud, like we did when we were kids. We've cracked jokes and listened to the sound of one another's laughter. Today, to us, nothing exists outside the boundaries of this car.

Kelsey presses a button on the radio. One of our favorite rock songs vibrates through the speakers. She lights two cigarettes and slips one between my lips. For the duration of the song, we intertwine our hands and sing the lyrics as loud as our voices allow.

As the words float from my mouth, I try to imagine what some of my college friends are doing at this moment. Are they at home, in their rustic New England towns, spending time with their own childhood friends? I wonder what sorts of things they do. Normal things. All-American things. I believe they are the sorts of things Kelsey and I will never have the chance to partake in.

I try to imagine some of my new friends doing what I am doing right now: driving across state boundaries, caught in a conversation too deep to really be understood, in search of an escape.

But an escape from what?

From illness?

From our pasts?

I wonder what it would be like to be one of those girls. To have the sort of innocence that, at age nineteen, I've already been stripped of for years. To have a sense of real normalcy in my life to cling to instead of all this. Which is when I finally realize: for Kelsey and me, this is normal. Conversations about pills. A constant fear of death. This is what we have grown accustomed to. And for a minute, this thought helps me feel at ease.

But years from now, after Kelsey is gone, I will try to erase this part of my life. I will hide reminders of my past self — photographs, certain t-shirts, the broken black glasses that were once like a second skin — and replace them with pearl earrings and delicate silk scarves. I will tell coworkers playful anecdotes about my childhood and conveniently leave out any details related to Kelsey. Inside, my heart will flutter as I try to muster the courage to tell them about her so that they can thus have a better understanding of me. As I try to muster the courage to tell them that the simple truth behind each of my stories is this:

Once upon a time, there lived a beautiful, misunderstood child, with glistening red curls that danced down her back, and she defined me. And no matter how hard I try to brush the thought of her away, she remains.

Because she is a piece of my past.

A piece of my present.

She is everything.

Because that girl is still a part of me.

The track ends and Kelsey touches the radio knob to search for a new song. I reach out my hand and stop her.

"Let's listen to it one more time," I say and light the tip of another smoke.

The song begins to play again and Kelsey takes hold of my hand.

"Look," she says, and from the corner of my eye, I can see a tear sliding down her face. "I've thought about this a lot, and I know I'm making the right decision. I mean, in all honesty, would you want to live your life knowing the only thing keeping you going was a jar of pills?"

I am quiet for a moment before I answer her truthfully.

"No," I say.

"Well, neither do I," she says, and her voice sounds more calm than it has in months. "I can get through this without pills. I can make myself better again."

The track ends. Kelsey occupies herself with the radio knob.

"Just promise me," she says, "that whatever happens, you believe everything will be okay."

"But I don't know that it will be," I say.

She looks at me. Her eyes are glassy.

"I need you to promise me that it will," she says and squeezes my hand.

I take a final drag, flick my cigarette out the window, and watch in the rearview as orange sparks dance across the black highway.

"Then it will," I say.

In the distance, an exit sign appears that points us back in the direction of home.

As I sit at this moment, my chest is tight. The bone beneath my breasts seems to stab my lungs. The page in front of me is blank. I feel an emptiness grow inside me, a hollow shell that expands and contracts, but never closes, never heals. A scar. No words come to my mind.

I fear I have forgotten her.

I want to say "I have lost," and have these few words be enough. To write them over and over again, and know that someone, somewhere, will read between the lines and understand. But I know life is never this easy.

A friend of mine received a phone call recently. It was one of those calls that came too late in the evening to be something good. I watched my friend's face go gray just seconds after she said, "hello." The tears came almost immediately.

I listened to my friend's muffled sobs. It was clear in that instant that any sense of happiness that previously lived inside her had died. As I watched her shoulders begin to round forward and listened to the guttural sobs that escaped her throat, I wondered if she felt the same sense of emptiness I felt. I recall in that moment envisioning the inside of my body. In my vision, my interior was vacant of healthy pink organs and streams of vibrant, jewel-toned blood. All I could see was a dormant field that concealed every emotion that ever lived inside me and showed no signs of ever sprouting back to life. But as I watched her snap her phone shut, I began to imagine my insides quickly budding with color, like a series of time-lapse photographs. I wrapped my arms around my friend and allowed her damp face to rest in the hollow of my neck. Finally, I believed, I had someone to relate to.

"That was my mother calling," she said. "They've put our dog to sleep."

I stroked my friend's back and gently pressed my lips to her hairline.

"I'm sorry," I said and then released my arms from her so she could be alone and begin to grieve.

"It's okay," she said. I couldn't help but notice that the whites of her eyes were already hidden behind thin webs of pink. "We had her for so long. The truth, though, is that she was old and sick. It'll take our family a little while, but I'm sure eventually my mom will bring a new puppy into the house again."

She exited the room still sniffling. I watched her disappear and felt my body begin to numb once more as it occurred to me that, one day in a not so distant future, she would have the ability to replace her lost loved one.

Inside my body my happy garden withered and died.

I close my eyes, listen to the soft, electronic buzz of my computer screen and think of Kelsey. I do not see her face, but rather, become enveloped in a feeling of what it was like before life began to change:

Summer. The heady scent of fresh grass clippings. Stinging, bloodshot eyes after hours in chemical blue pools. Dusk air laced with charcoal and chlorine. The zap of a Japanese beetle who meets her fate in a black-light trap.

Winter. Our lungs fill with biting cold. We lie on wooden toboggans, crisp air rushing against our cheeks, and slide onto the surface of a black, frozen lake. Don't jump too much or you'll form a crack. Break your mother's back. We catch snowflakes on our tongues.

Autumn. The wind paints our faces with natural rouge. We run barefoot through midnight fields, let the October breeze billow our hair, and describe who we hope to become and who we swear never to be.

I think about how I have become that person I swore never to be.

When the air is warm, we roam the streets of our town at two a.m. and belt out song lyrics. Windows of nearby homes illuminate with yellow squares of light. Kelsey and I hide behind manicured hedges and laugh into our palms. When we emerge, I lie in the center of the road, my spine aligned with a golden rectangular line. Kelsey jumps back and forth across my body, laughing furiously, while I stare at the sky and look for patterns in the stars. Not once do I think of traffic or other obvious dangers, because, in my heart, I believe we are safe here.

This is what it feels like to be home. This is what our lives used to be.

Every now and then, no matter how many times I wash, I swear I can still smell a trace of chlorine on my skin.

Christmas morning. I follow the trail of cookie crumbs and broken carrot bits — a childish tradition my parents have never had the courage to break — that lead from my bedroom door to my family's decorated tree. I touch my fingers to my favorite ornaments. A heavy, red fire truck. A papier-mâché globe. A ceramic sugar cookie. A burgundy glass ball. Tiny bulbs illuminate my hand with patterns of red, blue and green. I fall into a trance while I cradle a porcelain teacup that dangles from a flimsy branch.

Outside the window, snow begins to dust the ground. Or at least that is how it appears in my memory. Perfect fat flakes that float slowly from the sky and cover everything. I wrap my body in a crocheted blanket, cup my hands against the frosted glass and watch the world become hidden beneath a delicate layer of white. Life appears like a picturesque scene from inside a snow globe. Everything so quiet and so still. For an instant, I wonder when some phantom hand will come shake this flawless moment and provoke a storm.

My mother presses a copy of *It's a Wonderful Life* into the VCR. My father balances hearty plates of bacon and fried eggs in his hands. My sister and her boyfriend walk through the front door, multiple gift bags balanced on their arms. In moments, my sister and I revert to children and tear through packages, throw torn sheets of metallic paper above our heads, and watch with pleasure as ribbons and wrapping flutter to the carpet. I unwrap a blue angora sweater I will never wear. A long-sleeved thermal with feminine mother-of-pearl buttons on the sleeves. A pair of tailored khaki pants. My mother playfully sticks a metallic bow onto her head. My father pours a second helping of rich eggnog into our mugs. I toss crumpled sheets of paper to the sky, like confetti. In the background of our celebration, Jimmy Stewart's voice echoes as he contemplates the value of his life.

Evening. I lie across a high-backed sofa in my aunt's living room, my sister curled up beside me, surrounded by scraps of silver and gold wrapping, and listen to the crackle of firewood. The blue and orange flames warm my face and make my eyes heavy. Just before they fully close, through a wall of French doors, I glimpse the glittering white speckles of snow that accumulate against a backdrop of darkness.

Beside me, my phone quivers and flashes green.

"It's me," Kelsey says, her voice soft, almost a whisper. "Can I come by your aunt's place?"

I let out a long yawn and pull my body upright from its sleeping position.

"Yeah, of course," I say. "Is everything okay?"

"Everything is fine," Kelsey says, though something in the urgency of her voice prevents me from believing her. "I just really want to spend a part of the holiday with your family this year."

I snap the phone shut and let my body melt into the couch cushions once more. My sister breathes gently as she sleeps. Just as I begin to refocus on the winter scene, my phone vibrates in my hand.

"I'm sorry," Kelsey says. "I just can't."

"Wait, what?" I say and rub my eyes. "You can't what?"

"I just think maybe I'd better go to bed instead," she says.

"But why?" I say. "I thought you wanted to see everyone."

"I do," she says. "I just don't think I can tonight."

"Oh," I say. "Are you sure everything is okay?"

She is quiet for a moment.

"Did you see the snow?" she says, ignoring my comment.

I tilt my head and watch as white dust litters the ground.

"Yes," I say. "I'm watching it right now."

"Me too," she says. "It's nice, isn't it?"

There is a brief silence as we listen to each other's breath.

"You remember when we were little," she says, "and your parents used to take us sledding near the lake?"

"Yeah," I say. "I remember."

"That was really fun," she says and I hear soft muted sounds as she cries.

"You know, I bet they still have those toboggans packed away someplace. We should go again sometime," I say.

Through the window, I watch the snow fall and cover everything. Each flake accumulates into a tapestry that spreads across the yard. A thin veil of white conceals the ground, the metal patio furniture, and the few garden decorations that have been left outside. All that is left of the familiar scene are outlines.

"Tell your family I said thanks and that I love them. And tell everyone I said Merry Christmas," Kelsey says and then hangs up the phone.

No one in my family will ever see Kelsey again.

People often ask about her, as though I am a scholar on her life. When they do, the first thing I always offer, as though by instinct is, "She had red hair."

There are so many other, perhaps more interesting, things I could tell. That she aspired to be an artist or a writer. That she was an hourglass with green, neon eyes. I could talk about her foul mouth. Or the self-consciousness she cleverly masked with false confidence.

(In the summers, she swam in a t-shirt and cotton boxer shorts, self-conscious for the world to see her body.)

I could tell these people about the tattoos and piercings she acquired in the hopes of obtaining a new identity.

(Identities?)

I could discuss for hours the way she made the nuns in our catechism class scream and smack rulers in a fury when she tried to disprove the life of Jesus.

I could describe her fascination with Salinger and her hobby of scribbling the opening lines from *The Catcher in the Rye* across her notebooks and on sheets of paper she taped inside her closet doors...

But I never say any of these things. Instead, I simply mumble my rehearsed response — she had red hair — and go about my day.

Occasionally, I wonder why this is the detail I cling to. I wonder why I feel this brief description should explain it all.

Perhaps because out of the some six and a half billion people that inhabit our planet, only about two percent are natural born red heads.

Maybe I hope that, somehow, this single fact will neatly sum up all the other details.

I slip the wool hat from my head and unwind the knit scarf that is wrapped around my neck. Salsa music blares through the speakers of the restaurant, making me crave the summer months. Two girlfriends and I sit around a cobalt blue tiled table. I've known these girls for the better part of my life but, for the most part, have never been more than their acquaintance. However, since I've been away at school, these are the girls that Kelsey has begun to spend her time with — any of the time that she is willing to leave the confines of her purple room.

Crystal runs her fingers through her brunette bob, shaking away the subtle glisten of snowflakes. She vigorously rubs her palms together to warm them and rehashes the details pertaining to her recently completed term at the community college and some memorable anecdotes from her part-time waitress gig. Tiffany signals the server, a boy we know from grammar school, and slides a trendy, bejeweled cigarette case from her purse. She places a cigarette between her lips and then speaks briefly about her most recent relationship, impatiently tapping her fingers against the tabletop the entire time she speaks. Our server brings us a basket of warm tortilla chips and two pitchers of margaritas, despite the fact that we are all underage. Tiffany sloppily pours us each a generous serving, balances her cigarette on the rim of a plastic ashtray and indulges in a hearty sip.

"So, how is school?" she asks me and forces a smile. "What's it like to be someplace other than this shit town?"

I tell them about my British Literature class and describe the ivy growing up the outer walls of the academic buildings. I reach into my purse for an envelope of photographs and show them pictures of my roommates and my dorm. I tell them about the older boy I've fallen for. They let me have my moment. And then they shift the focus to Kelsey.

"We're so glad you're finally home," Tiffany blurts out. Crystal offers her a scathing expression.

"It's just that, well, Kelsey really seems to miss you," Crystal clarifies.

"I know she isn't doing well," I say and watch as they both visibly exhale sighs of relief. "I mean, obviously we all know she has been sick."

"Yeah, but has she always been like *this*?" Tiffany asks.

"What do you mean like *this*?" I ask. "Like, as serious as this?"

"She's getting much worse," Crystal admits. "I've never seen her this bad. She's not the same person she was last year. Christ. She's not even the same person she was last month."

"I feel like we're losing her," Tiffany says and tries to hide her obvious tears by tilting her glass to her mouth.

"I feel like we've already lost her," Crystal whispers.

They both look to me in the way I imagine daughters look to their mothers for advice.

"I don't know what to do," I finally say, tilt back my tumbler to finish my cocktail and immediately pour a second glass.

"She calls me all the time," I tell them. "We talk two, three, sometimes five times a day. I don't know what else I'm supposed to do to help her when I'm so far away."

"Did she tell you that she lost her job again?" Crystal asks in reference to yet another of Kelsey's part-time gigs. "First, there was the coffee shop. Then the bookstore. This is the third part-time job she has lost in the last few months. It's like, she wants to go, but she just won't get out of bed most days. Absolutely refuses. Her parents have totally reached their limit. I don't know what they're going to do."

"Even something as simple as this — sitting around and having dinner with friends — she won't leave her bed for," Tiffany adds. "I mean, even when *you're* here. She won't even get out of bed for you."

My cell phone rings. The conversation ceases. They both assume, based on my expression, that it is her.

"Hello?" I say.

"It's me," she says through sobs. "They kicked me out."

"What are you talking about, Kelsey? Who kicked you out?"

"My parents. They hate me. They don't want me here anymore. My father hates me because I don't have a job. He doesn't understand what I'm going through. He's sick of paying doctor bills. He hates me. Nobody understands."

"Where are you?" I ask.

"In my driveway," she says. "I'm going to go for a drive."

"Just wait there, Kel," I say. "I'm leaving now."

When the girls and I arrive at the house, each of us buzzed from tequila, Kelsey stands at the edge of the driveway. Her face is streaked with black lines of mascara-stained tears. Two bulky garbage bags rest at her sides. The girls wait on the sidewalk while I approach Kelsey.

"What's in the bags?" I ask.

"My stuff," she says. "I can't live here with them anymore. And anyway, even if I wanted to, they won't let me."

"I'm sure they didn't kick you out," I say. "It was probably just a heat of the moment type thing."

"They hate me," she says and stares at the ground. "Everyone does."

I wonder if what she says is true. Did her parents indeed kick their daughter — the same girl who is so obviously ill — out of their home? Despite all their faults I know her parents love her in the same way all parents love their children. Two narrow windows beside the front door are illuminated with light. I wonder what her parents are doing inside. Do they even know that Kelsey is standing out here, her wrinkled clothes tossed carelessly into two Hefty bags? Is it possible that they allowed her to walk out the door without expressing any signs of concern or remorse? Could it be that this really was their final straw? Even in times of sickness, I think, people are only equipped to handle so much before they snap. But still, I can't help but erase the question from my mind: did the three of them even get into an argument tonight at all? Or is this one of the final stories in Kelsey's invented string of lies?

"Come on," I say and begin to lift one of the bags. "Why don't you come home with me tonight? You can stay with my parents and me for a few nights while your parents cool off."

"I can't," she says.

"Of course you can," I say. "You know you can always stay there, even when I'm away."

"I just can't," she says again. "Not tonight."

"So where are you going to go?" I ask. "You can't just drive around all night."

Kelsey tells me that she plans to stay at a friend's house — someone who was once a casual acquaintance but who she has grown closer with in the months of my absence.

"Why don't I come there with you?" I suggest. "And then we'll figure out a more long term plan together in the morning."

"I just want to be alone," she says. "Will you help me bring these things to my car?"

I carry the two garbage bags filled with Kelsey's belongings and place them on her backseat.

"I'm sorry," she says and presses her face against my chest. Her sobs break the silence of the otherwise quiet winter night. "I'm really sorry for doing this to you."

"Please come home with me," I whisper. "Please don't go somewhere else."

Kelsey's cold, pale hands tenderly grip the sides of my head.

"I'm glad that you're home," she says and kisses my face.

While her lips press against my cheek, I gently grip one of her hands. As I do, my fingertips brush against the cool metal band that hugs her finger.

"See," I say through broken sobs. "It's just like you said, Kel. We've never really been apart."

Both of our bodies shiver as we stand only inches from each other, our gaze set eye-to-eye as tears slide down our cheeks and blur our vision.

"I'm sorry I left you," I say, suddenly ashamed of my collegiate path.

Kelsey tries to compose herself and begins to wipe the undersides of her eyes. I follow her to her car and lean my head through the window as she buckles her seat belt and lights a cigarette.

"Don't be sorry about leaving," Kelsey says. "I wish I could have left, too."

"I'm sorry," I say again through my sobs.

She clicks on the car radio and shifts her car into drive. I wrap my arms around my body and watch as her red convertible accelerates down the street, eventually turning a corner and disappearing from my sight forever.

The next morning, I am alone in my bedroom, sorting through gifts and cleaning up from the holiday. I unpack duffel bags of clothes from college and flip through textbooks. I eat a bowl of boxed macaroni and cheese.

The phone rings.

"Hey," she says and her voice sounds calm. "Look. I can't really talk long. I just wanted to call and let you know I'm heading to my sister's. I'm going to stay at her apartment for the night."

"Oh, okay," I say. "Do you want to come stay here instead? You know my parents won't mind."

"Not tonight," Kelsey says. "I'd rather stay someplace else actually."

There are things in life I will never be able to explain. Why the sound of crashing waves leaves me with a feeling of peace. Why, every so often, I experience déjà vu. Why, in the silence of my bedroom, I pray to an invisible God.

In this instant, I experience another of these mysteries. I finally begin to hear the meaning behind Kelsey's words. Something inside of me clicks on. The fog begins to lift. The scene is clear. All the confusion and uncertainty begins to thin.

And somehow, in my heart, for reasons I may never comprehend, I know this is the end.

I think of all the things I should do. I should call her mother. I should call the police. I should hang up the phone, get in the car myself, drive at the highest speed and try to save her. But then this thought comes to me: isn't that what we've all been trying to do for so long?

Here is a riddle: Two little girls grow up and become women. One of the girls is fine. But the other is sick. Very sick. And has been for a very long time. Maybe forever. And no amount of medical bracelets or encouraging words will make her sickness go away. She is ill and she is at her breaking point. So what is her friend to do?

"I know you're worried about me," Kelsey says. "But I'm going to be fine."

"I know," I say and pause.

Thousands of thoughts illuminate in my mind like flashing neon bulbs. I want so badly to tell Kelsey what she has meant to me. To tell her that she has inspired me and will continue to inspire me long after she is gone. To tell her that her face will forever live inside me. That, as an adult, I will see shadows and believe they are her.

I want to ask her to watch over me, and to give me strength to get through the battle I know I am about to face. To tell her that, for the rest of my life, I will keep a picture of her at my bedside, and, before drifting off to sleep, wonder if she is okay. If she is better than she once was.

I want to tell her I'm sorry for all the things I never did. For all the things I could never say. For being too young to understand when it was most important that I did. To tell her that, sometimes, in my twenties, I will drive for hours through snow and through rain just to see the church we used to attend. I will stare at the stone edifice, listen to the bells chime and wonder if she is in His care.

I want to tell her I will be angry for many years and will say things about her I really do not mean. *Selfish. Crazy.* That I will experience denial. That I will feel pain. That I will have panic attacks so severe that some days I will refuse to leave my bed. That my heart will ache long after she is gone.

But I am too afraid to admit the true intention of Kelsey's call.

"Look," Kelsey says. "I've got to go. I'm sorry." She releases a long, even-toned sigh. "I just need to get away for a few days."

"Kel — " I say, interrupting her.

I contemplate all the thoughts in my mind and try to find the courage to speak them. I open my mouth:

"I love you."

I pray these words are enough.

"I love you, too. I promise I'll see you real soon," she says and then hangs up the phone.

And as the line ends, and all I hear is white noise, I recognize that the sound of her final breath through my receiver will ring in my ears forever.

I think about death more than I should.

   I often find myself consumed by the idea of it. I look at my life, at the people that matter to me: my mother, father, friends, and wonder when they will die. I picture their hearts exploding in their chests, visualize their cars smashing, see them choking, struggling for air, watch films in my head of bullets piercing their skulls.

   I fear leaving these people. When it is time for a vacation, a road trip, a weekend get away, I panic. What if something should happen to them in my absence? What if something happens to me and they are all left to clean up my messes?

   I question my mortality. Obsess over when my time will run out. Will I have a chance to press my nose against the glass of a taxi and stare out at Les Champs-Elysees? Will I make love again, one last time, or is this it? The final chance.

   I recognize that I bring it upon myself. The little voice inside me constantly whispering that my breath might be growing short. That I am having an allergy to something, the food, the soap, the air, that my throat is closing. That my heart is slowing inside my chest, that it is failing and is out of my control.

   I have had friends roll eyes at me when I press my fingers against my neck at the dinner table to monitor my pulse. Have tapped their foot when I stop a conversation to inhale deeply and make certain my lungs are up to capacity. Have called me wasteful after I cook and throw away an entire meal before the first bite, suspicious of the meat, the eggs, the poultry that was bad and would have made me ill.

   I fear the people I care for will never know how much they really mean to me, and so I tell them, constantly. I love you. I love you. I make certain to tell them each time they walk down the steps, onto a plane, into their bedroom, out of my vision, a strange comfort knowing if we never meet again, my final words will bear weight. Mommy is going to bed. I love you. Daddy is off to run errands. I love you. Boyfriend leaves the room. I love you.

I love you…

I love you.

It was not always this way.

I used to attend church on Sundays. I used to believe in God and His power.

Some people say that, when loved ones die, they come to you in your sleep to let you know they are gone.

Many days I wake with no recollection of my dreams. I crawl from beneath my bed sheets and groggily move through my regimented morning routine. Scrub. Lather. Brush. Comb. I float through the house, hardly aware of my own movements until something — a smell or a song, maybe — reminds me. Fragmented scenes flash through my mind like forgotten memories. And, in an instant, the whole dream starts to unravel.

My head jolts from my pillow, my forehead beaded with perspiration and the pressing feeling that something heavy has been laid across my chest. I dab the dampness from my face and study the weaved pattern of my blanket before I drop my feet to the floor. In the bathroom, I splash handfuls of cool water across my face. In the kitchen, I prepare a mug of herbal tea. In the living room, I sit beside my mother and wander aimlessly through the channels, surfing my way through China, the weather in Los Angeles, and new and improved food processors, all in a blur.

"I feel like something is wrong," I say. "I had a bad dream."

My mother turns to me, rolls her eyes and lifts one side of her mouth into a half smile. She strokes her fingers through her hair, still flattened down from sleep.

"You're just being a hypochondriac," she says and shuffles towards the kitchen.

I continue to flip, robotically pressing my finger to the remote. Another game show. A teen romance movie. A news report. And then, something on the screen triggers it. A feeling overwhelms me. Without warning, I begin to remember:

An empty room, made of concrete. I am seated in a stiff-backed chair. She stands in front of me, her face different, not quite hers, but somehow, I know that it is. She tilts her head. I reach for her hand and caress her smooth, pale flesh. But in a flash, her body twists and she runs from me. Her fingers slip from my grip. I stand, but feel as though I am trapped underwater. My body struggles to move fast enough. I fall to the ground, scratch my fingernails across the stone floor, and try to crawl towards her. Just as I begin to make some headway, she disappears around a corner, and is gone.

Back in my bedroom, my body feels weightless. Before I can think about what I am doing, I start to tear pictures from my walls and situate them into an organized pattern across the floor:

A long row of pictures from elementary school.

(A photograph of our first grade Halloween parade. I am dressed as an angel and press a glitter wand to her head).

A long row of pictures from middle school.

(A photograph of us seated on a brick wall in Philadelphia, our middle fingers extended for the camera).

A long row of pictures from high school.

(A photograph of us standing on dark, dampened sand, our bodies positioned before a violent sea).

A short row of pictures from recent months.

(A photograph of her, dark circles beneath her eyes, puffy cheeks, an unfocused stare).

My eyes roam across these four distinct rows in an effort to find the beginning. But the beginning of what? Of our friendship? Of her illness?

My mother pushes my door open a crack and watches me as I frantically situate the photos.

"What are you doing?" she says. "You have to shower. Your father and I want to leave for New York in an hour. Your sister is already on her way into the city to meet us."

*Right*, I think. New York. A Broadway show. A day with family. I open my mouth and hope the right words will find their way out. A choice phrase to explain the anxious feeling that sits in my core.

My phone begins to shake out nervous vibrations and dance across the floor. I glance briefly at its illuminated square face and recognize the caller. But I don't need to answer. I already know what news the caller bears. The dream. That image of her running from me. Inside, I can feel it, though I'm not ready to hear it through the phone just yet. Instead, I look to my mother, say, *okay*, step across the mosaic of photographs, and out into the hall.

Outside the car window, sunshine melts snow into broken puzzle pieces. Sheets of it slip from car hoods and explode on the highway. In the distance, tunnels of light project from a mass of gray clouds, diagonal beams that shoot from the sky. My parents chatter nonsense, mindlessly discussing the holiday that has just barely passed. Their words seem to blend into muted noise. The only thing I hear is the muffled vibration of my phone; I take it in my hand with the intention of silencing it. Rather, I stare at its blinking green light and press it to my ear.

A friend. A phone call. Police. A body. Pills. Her sister's bed. Goodnight. It's over. She's gone.

I'd rather stay someplace else actually.

The car rolls forward. Tires rush through puddles of slush. Silver clouds swirl artfully in the winter sky.

I tuck my phone into my coat pocket. My fingers tingle as my body begins to numb.

It will be years until I feel anything more than this again.

I wonder if it is true, what they say. That, in the second before you die, your entire life flashes before you. In a split-second, the memories pour like waterfalls into your head and trickle like streams through your veins. Every detail, every instant you thought was forever lost floating in the peaks and valleys of your mind, is reborn. And, just for a moment, as your final breath escapes you, you remember what it was like to live.

I think about her final seconds and speculate whether or not I was a mere droplet or a roaring rapid that pulsed through her.

Our childhood Halloween parades, when we marched beside one another all through town.

The nights we sat and smoked cigarettes together until dawn.

The day the sky broke into pieces and sent lightening into the waves. (We danced across the sand and let the storm drip down our backs.)

I speculate if I was the final liquid bead that pulsed through her body. Or if I was lost somewhere inside her, trying desperately to find my way upstream.

A few months before the end, I stood at Kelsey's bathroom mirror and smoothed red lipstick across my lips. Kelsey sat on her bedroom floor, just across the hall from where I stood, her legs tucked beneath her behind. She wore a red t-shirt with the words "Hum Machine" written in script across the chest.

I don't recall what Kelsey was doing at that moment. Folding clothes? Puffing a cigarette? Sorting through old albums? I probably never will. I do remember, though, that she looked like a child seated on the floor that day. Her skin was free from makeup, and her fingers innocently fiddled with something on the ground, the way an infant might become preoccupied with a toy. I called out her name. She turned to me and smiled. I blinked and, just like that, snapped a photo of her in my mind. By the time my eyes reopened, she had already turned away. I smoothed on a second coat of red.

When I close my eyes and hope for the world to disappear, this image of Kelsey appears to me against a screen of darkness — a splotchy vision of her face that throbs in my eyes, the way sunspots do.

I often wonder what she felt during those final seconds. If there was a sense of peace found in the knowledge that it was all coming to an end. If there was fear or anger or regret. If she saw my face, and, in it, found a wave of comfort, a sense of peace. If the scenes of her life ebbed and flowed through her body one final time…

Or if it is all just some myth.

If she just closed her eyes that night and slipped quietly into a sea of blackness.

It's not often that one imagines what his or her reaction to death might be. In fact, I've never really imagined it at all. However, if someone had told me beforehand that today would be the day she would leave me, I imagine my reaction would have been something like this: a mixture of sweat and tears saturating my skin as I haphazardly throw heavy objects at a wall, knees pressed against my chest while I weep. But right now, just seconds after I have hung up the phone, all I feel is calm. Just moments ago, I informed my parents (who are now frantic in the front seat, my mother's face drenched in emotion) in a collected and even-toned voice:

You'll have to turn the car around. Kelsey died last night.

But now, as this life-altering information hovers around the three of us like a cloud of humid air, I cannot help but sit and peacefully gaze out the window. All I can think is what a lovely day it is outside. The sun shines with a golden glow. Beams of yellow light break through gray winter clouds. Cars race past in a sort of unplanned parade. The sides of the highway glisten with puddles of oil and melting snow.

In my head, I repeat the Hail Mary, as though it is a song. I watch car tires spin through dirty slush and imagine the beat of my prayer is what makes them move. In my mind, I tell myself, it is what makes us all move. And somehow, for the moment, this makes the whole mess of things seem okay.

When our car turns into Kelsey's drive, I do not rush out and wave my arms in frenzy. There are no rivers of tears that stream down my cheeks. Inside my head, where one might imagine are a muddle of manic thoughts, are only rational ones instead. I purposefully stop, tap my boots against the edge of the doorframe and watch snow clumps fall from the cuffs of my pants. I pause to apply some cherry lip stain. I lick my fingers and smooth strands of my hair.

I open the door to the house and hear its interior scream with silence.

I float up the entry stairs and into the kitchen, where her immediate family sits, and instinctively lift my bottom onto the countertop. From up here, on my private perch, I study their grief. Hands cupped over already swollen eyes. Void expressions on somber faces. Shoulders that shake with sobs. I try to keep my attention focused on these things — the piles of crumpled tissues, the blank stares — though my eyes betray me. They repeatedly wander to the singular thing in the room that actually disturbs me: one vacant seat at an otherwise full table. Her seat, left empty.

And with this, the bitter truth of today slowly begins to sink in.

In the next room, an electronic train set still circles a track that lies at the foot of a synthetic Christmas tree. In my head, I continue to repeat the Hail Mary.

Pray for us sinners now and at the hour of our death.

Amen.

Finally, her mother stands. Her fragile body is more fragile today than I've ever seen it. She leans in close to me and says something, though I hardly hear her words. All I notice is the fact that, today, there is no scent of alcohol on her breath. I'd like to tell her that, of all days, this would be the one to pour a nice, stiff drink. She looks like she needs one. I want to tell her that I need one, too. I'd like to reach into the cabinet behind me, the one where I know she keeps an extra stash, wrap my lips around the rim of a bottle and let my throat burn until it is the only thing left that I can feel. But instead, I wrap my arms tight around her frail frame and whisper, *we're all going to be okay.*

Kelsey's mother pulls herself from my embrace.

"I'd like you to be the first to sort through her things," she says, grips my arm and escorts me towards Kelsey's bedroom.

Kelsey's things are in the same organized clutter as always, and I cannot help but wonder if she planned it this way. If she took a moment to hide certain belongings. If she made the effort to leave certain things in plain view. Or if, somehow, this whole thing *was* an accident. If she closed her door with the intention of, at some point, returning.

It is something I will contemplate forever.

I settle onto the carpet and her mother gently closes the door.

From my place on the floor, I let my eyes wander and observe the tiny mementos from my friend's short life. The photographs. The stacks of CDs. The pieces of art. And suddenly, before I even have the chance to realize she is gone, I am alone with her all over again. Her scent pours from everything: her blankets, still twisted from a night of restless sleep. Her piles of dirty laundry, tossed throughout her room.

In the hall, I hear the shuffle of footsteps. More friends have arrived. I cannot help but think that, out there, just past that closed door, is a world where she is gone, but that, in here, inside the confines of this purple room, she is still alive. Her imprint remains on everything. Her tattered denim jacket that still hangs from her bedpost. Her half drunk cup of iced tea, her lip prints still on the rim of the glass. The whole room reeks of her. And as I begin to take in her life just hours after it has passed, I cannot help but think of the irony of the whole situation: that here, inside the boundaries of the room that tried to swallow her, she is now most alive.

I let my face fall to the floor and breathe in her smell like it is a drug. I know that, in just a few days, this scent will fade. That, for the rest of my life, I will sample perfumes and lotions from across the globe in an effort to find something similar to it, though never will. There is no way to replace a human scent. Over the years, it simply becomes too complex. She smells like everything to me. Honeysuckle and cigarettes. Midnight air and hospital beds. I think of the fact that, soon, I won't ever have the opportunity to smell her again.

I turn onto my side and notice a heap of journals beneath her bed. I know that if I flip through their pages, I will find the answers I am looking for. A reason. A meaning. A layer of truth behind it all. But I'm hardly ready to ask these questions, let alone discover their answers. It will be years before I am ready for that, and, even then, will question if I am ready at all. Instead, I reach my arm towards her bed, pull a blanket from the mattress, and wrap it around my body and the lower half of my face. Beneath the weight of it, my body struggles to move. My chest has difficulty expanding. These thoughts are too heavy right now. I have become mummified, trapped beneath her quilt, her smell, and her new reality: the one in which she is gone.

Right now, the only thing I can do is envelope myself beneath this fabric and observe the four walls that surround me. My eyes shift and study the tiny memories that hang from the walls, as though I am in some twisted gallery space. But no thoughts come to me. My body is trapped. My lungs feel as though they are collapsing. My whole sense of self is gone. I feel more alone, right now, than I have ever imagined was within human capacity.

In this moment, I begin to understand fear. I begin to understand desperation. I begin to understand the allure of wanting to stay still and stare blankly at purple walls.

And for the first, and perhaps only time, I begin to understand how she felt all along.

The road is lined with snow where I am used to seeing sand. Chilled December air rushes through the car. Kelsey's final arrangements ended only hours ago. Tiffany's boyfriend drives the car while Crystal and other acquaintances fill the remaining seats. My hair whips across my face. My skin feels frosted and numb. I pinch myself. For a moment, I do not believe I am alive.

The breeze whistles in my ears as the car twists through blackness, maneuvering narrow, winding curves. I lean my head against the open window frame. In silence, I watch flat, winter fields roll past like black and white snapshots — the whiteness of the winter moon reflected onto a tapestry of snow, a black sky flecked with gray. The world around me is frozen.

There are no more words.

The services have just barely ended, and, yet, I hardly recall them. I only remember fragments:

A crowd in black. Her vacant body at rest in a satin-lined bin. The glint of the silver ring on her finger. The smooth feeling of my own ring as I absently caressed it with my fingertips. The idea that the rings would somehow keep us connected. The chill of holy water being splashed against my skin. The man beside me who held my hand. The yellow rose I dropped into the earth. Wondering if she could feel the weight of it on her chest. If she could smell the dampness of the soil that surrounded her. Wondering if she was there with me. Knowing I was there alone.

It had all been too much. I had to get away. Friends began to pile into a car. I followed them. A drive to the shore at three a.m.

Music screams through static speakers and vibrates me to my core. Years from now, when I think back on this moment, I will not remember what song had been playing; only that its lyrics made me cry.

The car rolls into a gravel lot. No one has the spirit to move from the car. I crawl out alone and sit on the warm, rattling hood. Above me, I notice the licorice sky, speckled with white. My eyes wander down to the rounded dunes, the patches of swaying sea grass, and the whitecaps of waves. I light a cigarette. The black sea is dark. Endless. Still. It makes me think of her. I exhale a warm cloud of smoke and then toss the cigarette to the ground. There is a void growing inside me. I slide off the hood. The car reverses and turns around just as quickly as it came.

I tilt my head and watch the passing, familiar landscapes through the window:

The golf green, illuminated by a silver moon.

The stretches of frozen fields, hidden beneath a blanket of snow.

The farmhouse, with its strings of multicolored holiday lights.

There they go.

The scenes of so many years.

The scenes of my childhood.

Goodbye.

I breathe deep and try to absorb them all one final time. My plan fails me.

"I feel like I can't breathe," I whisper. "I feel like my insides are all ice."

No one in the car has the heart to speak. They are each consumed with their own numbness.

"I can't breathe," I say again.

But still, there is only the sound of silence.

I clutch my throat and lower my jaw.

It is difficult to describe the sound of a scream. It seems a cross between something like glass shattering, an unexpected burst or explosion, and a baby crying, a loud release of beautiful sound. I throw my face between my knees and let the noise rip from my core, shake through the silence of the car, and disrupt the peacefulness of this otherwise calm, winter night.

Someone strokes a hand across my back.

"Get off me," I say. "You have to get your hands off me."

*Why did you do this to me?*

"I think I'm dying," I say. "Somebody please do something. Does anyone hear me?"

*Do you hear me?*

The car swerves to the shoulder and I roll out feeling weightless. My back pressed against the door, my body slides to the earth. Frozen salt tracks crust down my cheeks. The taillights flash red bursts in the snow. I watch them pulse and think of a heartbeat. I think of her heart beating and then ceasing. All around me, delicate flakes calmly flutter towards the ground.

By the time I climb back into the car, my legs are all pins and needles from the cold. I breathe deep and press my fingers to my wrist. I feel the blood beat through my veins. For perhaps the first time in my life, I am disheartened to know I am, in fact, alive.

I crawl across bodies and back into my seat. My breath begins to return to a steady rhythm. And then, as I slide over the last set of thighs, I glance through the frosted window to the opposite side of the road.

"You must be kidding," I say and continue to crawl right out the door.

Concealed behind the faint glow of blinking holiday lights is a barley legible sign hidden beneath a sheet of snow. I run towards it, frigid dampness soaking up my pant legs to my knees. The snow crunches in my fist as I mold it into an icy ball. When it makes contact, the snow slides from the sign and smashes onto the ground. The wooden sign swings back and forth, as though to summon me inside.

Blackberry wine.

Blackkkberryyy Wiiiiine.

My knees collapse and send my body crashing. My words are all trapped inside me, as though frozen in blocks of ice. And then, it comes again. The scream. Uncontrollable. A beautiful symphony of sound. I melt into the earth and sob to the glistening drifts of snow.

"What does this mean?" I whisper to the ground.

A rush of footsteps sound behind me. Hands randomly clutch at my body and pull me back in the direction of the car. I kick my feet in a manic anger and send dusty clouds of snow into the air. The icy particles swirl back down in a frantic storm.

The car rolls forward. Someone touches the volume knob and

music throbs through my head once more.

A hand rests itself upon my knee.

"Had you been to that place before?" a voice gently says.

*You know we'll never get to go.*

"No," I say. "I never went. I missed my fucking slot."

I press my face against the chilled glass and watch the silent, empty fields and endless black sky slide past me. In an instant, the frozen vineyard disappears into the darkness.

I dream about that church. The slippery pews with their padded kneelers. The marble baptismal basin, filled with blessed water, always so still and so cool to the touch. The rows of organ pipes that hung from the walls like a scene from the Emerald City. The golden censer that released curls of fragrant smoke towards the heavens.

Lord, hear our prayer.

Some nights, I dream that I am floating. I soar over the top of the aisle and glide over rows of tilted heads, bodies that kneel in prayer. I move, fluidly, past rows of windowpanes, all splashed with color, as though crayons have been melted and smoothed across the glass. The crucifix hangs before me, bronzed droplets of blood that drip down His body. I reach out my hand to touch His scars and everything goes white. My body lowers, and, for a moment, I believe I am weighted and sinking beneath the sea. I look up and see abstract bursts of sun. Any second, I am certain my toes will graze a smooth bed of sand.

When I land, I am a child, wearing white patent leather shoes. My feet click softly against the ground. You, too, are a child. You stand beside me, in your white dress and lace veil, red curls cascading down your shoulders and back and across your face. You take hold of my hand and we giggle at our ruffled, fold over socks and flat bellies. The sound of our laughter trickles through the place like droplets of cool, summer rain.

"I can be your angel," you whisper to me and your face fills with light. The gleam ricochets off the windows, illuminating biblical images of purple veiled women and lambs. It scatters patchworks of color across the floor.

"Are you ready?" you say and let my hand slide away from yours.

You place the small, papery wafer onto the tip of your tongue.

The body of Christ.

"I am afraid," I say.

You brush your delicate, child fingers across my cheek and they warm me.

"Don't be afraid," you say and smile. "It tastes just like Jesus."

I close my eyes, part my lips, and allow you to place His body into my mouth, where it turns moist and dissolves. When my eyes reopen, goldenness pours through the room, bursting from every crevice, like glimmering pieces of ice on a winter morning. Like Christmas morning, when I was very young. I let my eyes follow the miniature rainbows that dance across the ground, across the altar, and across His face. Your laughter echoes through the place like birdsong. And just like that, you are gone.

But sometimes, you are still there, and you touch my fingertips, and, like magic, we float together to an empty back pew. Our thighs touch and I can feel you, can feel your energy there beside me. It nearly takes my breath away.

We scan the rows of filled pews, bodies draped in black, like shadows. A group of men stand near the altar, their faces blurred masks of gray, as though some phantom eraser has smudged their mouths and cheeks. They clutch your final resting box in their hands.

"I can't watch," I say and lean my damp face against your breast.

The men's footsteps thud against the floor like lead pounding concrete. The flat, heavy sound reverberates through my core.

You press your fingers to my chin and lift my face; you are no longer a child, but a girl of thirteen, your hair the color of sweet autumn hay, your eyes like two slabs of jade.

"I wish you looked like this in the end," I say and you nod.

The footsteps sound closer, the noise so loud I think my ears will burst into pieces, like confetti. Before they do, the men reach the end of the aisle. The church's heavy wooden doors creak open.

"You're going to go now, aren't you?" I say and you nod again.

The men slowly march through the doorway and carry your resting box away from me. I drop my face into my palms and listen to the sound of their footsteps echo into the distance. When I lift my face, the room is silent. I can hear my heartbeat pump inside my throat. I turn from side to side and see the place has emptied. The lights have all been dimmed. You have disappeared and this time, I know it is for good.

On some rare nights, I dream of that final day. I stand inside a pew, a woman at age nineteen, wearing my fitted black skirt and mustard-colored sweater. I purchased the sweater thinking it would bring sunshine into the room. Now, in my dream, I wish I could tear the sweater from my chest, rub my heel into the cotton and make it go away. I want it all to go away. I open my mouth to scream but there is no sound — only bubbles, as though I am trapped at the bottom of a deep, dark sea.

The faceless men begin to march down the aisle once more, their shiny black shoes clomping against the ground; the sound becomes louder with each step they take towards me. Without warning, they abruptly stop beside my pew.

I reach out my hand and swipe it across your metal box. Tears spill from me. The salt sting burns so badly I can only narrow my eyes into slivers. The world is blurry and so I dab my swollen lids. That's when I see us seated together in a pew just a few rows ahead. We are thirteen years old and wearing our crisp, white confirmation gowns. I listen closely and hear our voices as we adlib song lyrics that mock the life of Christ. *God is good, but should smoke some weed. It'd be better if He didn't take life so seriously.* A nun hobbles towards us and slaps her hand against the wooden pew.

"But it's true," you say. "You *can't* take things like this too seriously."

When I look down beside me, I see that your coffin has sprung open. Your body is inside, your hair clipped close to your head and dyed such a dark shade of ebony that it nearly shines blue. Your face is bloated, pale, sick. Your body lies like a statue, like a piece of masked beauty frozen in time. Your hands are neatly folded across your chest, the silver band you were buried in hugging your finger.

It nearly takes my breath away.

I close my eyes and try to imagine you running, your body so animated and so alive. I try to imagine you at age thirteen with a wanderlust sparkle in your eyes…

And that's when I hear it — the guttural sound of your laughter. I open my eyes. Your head is tilted towards me, your eyes sprung wide, your finger pointed at my face.

Through a grin, your corpse laughs at my tears.

There is a Zen proverb that states, "No snowflake ever falls in the wrong place." As I sit here now, the echo of the doctor's voice in my ears, I think of the proverb and wonder if it is true.

I try to tell myself there is meaning in everything. That there is a purpose behind every tear, every laugh, and every storm.

I try, desperately, to find what the purpose of all this has been.

Some nights, when I cannot sleep, I stare at the smoothness of my ceiling and think of her. I imagine her strawberry blonde curls brushing against her back as she sprints before me through lush fields of corn. Yellow sunlight filters through the husks and illuminates her skin. In my mind, Kelsey turns to me and smiles. Her face consumes me, like an apparition. I remind myself of the proverb and make believe she is okay. I remind myself that we both ended in the places we were meant to land.

It is a hard idea to swallow.

There are days when the guilt is so severe I feel paralyzed. For hours, I sit and stare at nothing and relive moments from her life in my head. *How did I let this happen? Why did I not understand and intervene?*

I try to remind myself I was a child then. That my heart was too big and my comprehension of so many things still too small. I try to develop the courage to get past the blame.

The summer I turned seventeen, I joined Kelsey on a family vacation. On an afternoon towards the end of our trip, Kelsey and I walked across the small beach town where we were staying. We stopped into a local surf shop, purchased souvenir t-shirts and puka shell necklaces, and then found our way back onto the street. Within a matter of minutes, the sky changed from blue to gray to black. There was a violent roar, as though a knife had been sliced through the clouds.

The rain was blinding.

In just seconds, our shirts became translucent. Steam rose from the pavement. Kelsey and I kicked off our shoes and splashed through oily puddles, their surfaces shimmering with rainbows. We laughed and let the storm slide down our backs. Our mouths sprung open, we caught the rain on our tongues, like snowflakes.

When we returned to the small home Kelsey's parents were renting, rather than go inside and towel off, Kelsey and I walked the extra block to the beach. The sand was saturated. The ocean was choppy with white caps. Waves angrily slapped the shore and were sucked back to sea.

The place was deserted, except for us.

"Once, when I was little," Kelsey said, "I got pulled underneath. I had been swimming near the shore and a wave forced me under. I swallowed mouthfuls of saltwater. I couldn't catch my breath. Every time I tried to swim to the surface, another wave slapped me down."

A young couple emerged on the beach. They approached Kelsey and me to discuss the passing rain. As they spoke, I reached into my bag and pulled out a disposable camera I had forgotten about during the storm. The cardboard was soggy and I feared the film would be destroyed. I handed it to them. Kelsey and I moved closer to the water and let the tide brush over our feet. The wind blew our hair across our faces and we laughed while trying to push it away. Kelsey wrapped her arm around my shoulder. We smiled as the picture was snapped.

Long after the couple left, Kelsey and I remained on the beach and watched as the grayness of the sky began to break apart into a lavender web. I pulled the camera from my bag and fingered its dampened sides.

"Do you think it's ruined?" I said.

Kelsey shook her head. For moments, we stood side by side and admired the waves.

"As a kid," I said, "I always thought the ocean went on forever. When I looked out to the horizon line, I couldn't imagine that was the place where it would end."

In silence, we looked out to the spot where the sky melded with the sea.

"Maybe it does go on forever," Kelsey said. "Maybe the waves don't ever really have an end."

Kelsey took the camera from me, positioned it against her face, and looked out towards the water.

"Isn't it weird," she said, "how calm things can seem after a storm?"

I nodded to her. She clicked the final picture on the roll and then placed the camera back into my bag.

And just like that, we turned around and made our way across the sand.

When we returned from our trip, I thought the camera was lost. For months I searched for it, tearing through duffel bags and dresser drawers. It was not until long after Kelsey was gone that the camera found its way back into my hands.

I had the film developed immediately. Tears slid down my face when I viewed the still images of our bronzed skin, the snapshots of us laughing, the bottles of beer held to our lips. In the photographs, life seemed so carefree. Shortly after they were taken, Kelsey was admitted for one of her many hospital stays.

I flipped through the pictures slowly, taking in every detail of our smiles and our tan lines, before I reached the final photo:

A smooth ocean, framed by two crests of waves. A mass of wispy gray clouds, and, behind them, fragments of a clear, turquoise sky.

*Isn't it weird how calm things can seem after a storm?*

I wait for the day when this storm will finally pass.

The doctor places down her pad and pen.

"So why do you think you made yourself come here today?" she says and looks at me with kindness in her eyes.

I can provide the doctor with so many reasons. I can tell her I came here to try to remember. Or, perhaps, more honestly, that I came here to try to forget. I breathe deep.

"Because I haven't admitted it yet," I say and tilt my face to the ground.

Shortly after Kelsey died, there was a blizzard. It was night and I was alone driving on a stretch of highway in search of solitude. In an instant, fat, glistening flakes began to rush toward the windshield. I flicked on my high-beams. The world transformed into a tunnel. In front of me were only blurred streaks of white and darkness. I squinted but could not clearly see the world that existed just inches from me. My breath shortened. I clicked on the stereo, hoping to find comfort in a song. As its melody rang through my head, I wondered if the sense of disorientation and fear I felt was similar to what plagued Kelsey all along.

The doctor clears her throat.

"Admitted what?" she asks.

I think about my body. About Kelsey's body. About the cuts. I think about the fact that I will never heal from her. She is too much a part of me. She is my scar. Forever, she will be the scarlet slash that runs across my skin.

I push up my sweater sleeve and look down at the raised white scar that marks my wrist.

"That she is gone," I say.

When I graduate from college and begin to plan out my life, I think back on my childhood pact with Kelsey.

*Promise me that one day, we'll make it there. That we'll make it to New York.*

And so, rather than join friends on European vacations or cross-country road trips, I head to the one place I believe I really belong.

I land a job. I make friends. We eat dinners at Chumley's and stumble tipsily down Morton Street. I have Friday night martinis and Udon noodles in Union Square. I visit galleries and wear pointy-toed shoes and dresses with mature hemlines. I fall in and then quickly out of love with a man who lives on the Upper West Side. He takes me on a date and, afterwards, grants my request and walks me through Times Square.

"You know, this is the worst hour of the week to be here," he says, grabs hold of my hand and increases his speed. "Too many people," he says. "Too much noise."

I squeeze his palm and pause, ignoring his comments. Instead, I tilt back my head and smile, intoxicated by the glowing gardens of neon.

This is my new life: I dine on pâté in Williamsburg, Brooklyn. I count *three, two, one* on the Upper East Side, dance through a confetti storm, and kiss a man whose name I never ask. I have cab rides at four a.m. and subway rides at seven a.m. I have a desk with a leather picture frame and business cards that read, *New York, NY 10011.*

On a winter morning, I wake, my pulse thudding, after having dreamt of her. I crawl from bed, stand beneath the showerhead and breathe deep the steam. I rub my hand across the fogged mirror but only see her face. My mind is consumed with an image of her.

I walk to work. The busy sounds of the morning help me to momentarily forget her. I sip my coffee. I tuck a copy of the paper beneath my arm. I glance up and smile, pleased with the sight of a crystal sky.

The promise of an early spring.

But while crossing Fifth Avenue and Twenty-First Street, something in that flawless, periwinkle sky makes me remember. Her face floods my vision. The coffee falls from my grip. I am a statue, a cement silhouette in the street, oblivious to the honking taxis, the drilling of construction, the crowd that marches around me as though I am a ghost. I watch the brown liquid spill from the cup and spread across the pavement in streams.

My foot touches the curb. I pause and study my reflection in a shop window, the translucent image of my eyes aligned with the blurred cityscape. I stare back at myself for minutes, as though waiting for the reflection of her face to appear beside mine. For her fingers to caress my shoulder. For her to mock me for having had such a foolish dream.

But when Kelsey does not appear, the truth pummels me: she will never walk around a corner; she will never be on the other end of my office phone; she will never hop a subway, or skim prints at a corner vendor, or sit on a roof deck and admire the sight of a silver skyline against a backdrop of stars.

Before a year is up, I leave my life in New York. I fear the tunnels might spring a leak. That the bridges might all collapse. I fear the whole island of Manhattan might come loose and float someplace far away.

Some days, when the thought of missing her is too much to bear, my mother suggests I write a new story. One in which Kelsey makes it in the end.

I like to think my version of the story goes something like this:

The story begins when we are children. Kelsey and I spend our days in leisure and roam through wild, overgrown fields. We collect handfuls of honeysuckle and suck the sweet droplets from their centers. In the evenings, our skin smells of chlorine and too many hours spent in the sun. Each night, before drifting off to sleep, Kelsey softly kisses her mother's cheek.

"I love you," Kelsey whispers in her mother's ear.

Her mother returns the sentiment in clear, coherent words. In my story, her breath smells only of buttercups.

As my story progresses, Kelsey and I transform from girls into women. To celebrate, we drink bottles of blackberry wine until our mouths and teeth are stained purple. We dance, drunk and barefoot, through summer fields and laugh until our cheeks become damp from tears.

In the morning, we wake, our bodies spread across an expanse of lawn. In a moment of inspiration, we decide it is time to wave goodbye to the fields and the small streets we have called home for so many years. Together, we venture into the big city, where we decorate our roof deck with strands of tiny white lights. Each night, we stand beneath their glow, our waists pressed against the concrete edge of our building, as we admire the silver and charcoal skyline.

And all around us, we see neon.

# Acknowledgements

I am sincerely blessed to have had so many people support this project. Thank you to my mother for reading the early drafts, for encouraging me to continue writing each time I was about to give up, and, of course, for all the childhood library trips. Every woman should be fortunate enough to have a father who, with genuine interest and concern, listens to his daughter's dreams and then does everything in his power to help her make them her reality. Endless thanks to my husband for being so patient and so kind; I cannot imagine spending my life with someone who does not understand or appreciate the all-consuming power of the creative process. I will always be grateful for my college girlfriends who, during my darkest days, selflessly picked me back up, put me back together and taught me how to laugh and to live again. A very special thanks to Tom Kennedy and Walt Cummins – two inspiring mentors, talented writers and irreplaceable friends. I must also acknowledge Greg Bottoms, a fantastic teacher who first introduced me to the genre of creative nonfiction when I was an undergraduate and, without realizing it, managed to change the course of my life. Thank you to the publications who printed early drafts of several chapters included in this book: *Damselfly Press, Dislocate, In Our Own Words: A Generation Defining Itself, A Long Story Short, Lost, Miranda Literary Magazine* and *The Sylvan Echo*. Lastly, to the many individuals who experienced this part of my past with me: you know who you are. Eternal thanks for all the memories. The late night drives. The shared cigarettes. The bottomless mugs of diner coffee. I wouldn't be myself without them.

 Angela M. Graziano's essays, poems and interviews have appeared in multiple print and online publications including *Apple Valley Review, Ariel, Damselfly Press, Design\*Sponge, Diverse Voices Quarterly, Lost, Portal Del Sol, The Sylvan Echo*, and *Talking Writing*, among others. Additionally, her writing has earned her an artist grant from the Vermont Studio Center, where she was a writing resident in the summer of 2010.

She has conducted research for major print publications such as *In Style* and *In Style Weddings* and has served as a reader for *The Literary Review*. She has a Bachelor of Arts Degree in English from the University of Vermont and a Master of Fine Arts Degree in Creative Nonfiction Writing from Fairleigh Dickinson University. She lives, writes, and teaches in Morristown, New Jersey.

Her website is www.angelamgraziano.com.

Made in the USA
Lexington, KY
23 March 2013